The Detective's Forbidden Temptation

Copyright

Opening Quote

Your parents say everything is your fault, but they don't know you like I know you. They don't know you at all.

I'm so sick of when they say, "It's just a phase. You'll be okay. You're fine."

But I know it's a lie. This is the last night you'll spend alone. Look me in the eyes so I know you know. I'm everywhere you want me to be. The last night you'll spend alone. I'll wrap you in my arms, and I won't let go. I'm everything you need me to be. The last night away from me. The night is so long when everything's wrong. If you give me your hand, I will help you hold on. Tonight.

The Last Night by Skillet

Chapter One

☾★ Xavier ★☾

"What is this?" my father asks me. I close my eyes and take a deep breath, but don't turn around.

My father.

Such a fucking asshole.

I'm sure a lot of eighteen-year-old high school students say that, but my father really is an asshole. He's a detective with the Brystone Springs Police Department. Not that he wasn't always a cocky douche, but I think when he became a detective, his arrogance got a lot worse. He turned into an even bigger jerk.

His recent tirade against me, and believe me, there have been many over the years, is that I refuse to choose his beloved university. I don't have any fucking desire to go to Texas A&M, even though I've been recruited by their football team. I'm the best quarterback in the state, rivaling even college quarterbacks with my stats.

I'm good. I know I am. It's the entire reason colleges across the country have offered me full-ride scholarships and a fuck load of perks. One of them even said I'd have off campus housing, all paid for, and be an automatic addition to the most prestigious frat on campus. I looked into the frat. Those that are members get all the pussy they can handle, like I care about that anyway, and literally everything else a person can dream of. They rule the campus. I don't want any part of them. I chose my college long ago.

Much to the dickfuck's dismay.

I'm attending Brystone University. It's the second largest school in the State of Texas, and one of A&M's biggest rivals. Choosing them wasn't a coincidence. I like that they're a rival of my dad's fucking college, but I like even more that it's near Brystone. It's just outside of the city, but it's far enough away that I can start my own life while still being a part of the community I've grown to love. Brystone Springs isn't bad. The city can't help that my father is a part of it.

I lean back in my desk chair and rub my head. "What?" I grit out through my teeth.

"What? You know what," he growls. He slams an acceptance letter down on my desk on top of my history book. "What the fuck, Xavier? You're going to A&M."

I sigh. "Dad, we've been through this."

"We have. And I don't give a shit what you want. I worked my ass off to get you into A&M."

I raise an eyebrow as I stand slowly. I face him down. It's not the first time I've stood eye to eye and toe to toe with my father. I'm six feet two. He's the same. We share the same dark hair and silver eyes. We even share the same build. Toned and muscular.

"*You* didn't do shit. *I* got myself into every single one of the colleges I've been accepted to. *I'm* the one who busted my ass getting good grades while leaving it all on the field. Not *you*."

My dad shoves me backwards onto my bed. "Listen up, you little fucking punk. I'm not paying for you to go to any other fucking college but the one we've worked towards your whole life. For once, do what you're told."

I just glare. I don't move. I've played this game before. I might match my dad in looks, physical strength, and agility, but there's one thing he will always have on me.

His cop training.

He knows how to take down even the best fighters and toughest criminals without breaking a sweat.

5

"I don't want to go to Texas A&M. You can't force me. I'm an adult."

My dad chuckles and looks around my room. "An adult. Who lives under my roof. Drives a car I bought. Has a video and gaming system that came from my pocket. A nice ass TV in his room. Bed. Clothing. Furniture. All in my house. All because of me. You're an adult? Bullshit you are." I watch as he tears up the acceptance letter that he opened and slammed on my desk. I don't really care where it's from. I already have the acceptance letter from the University I'll be attending.

"Whatever," I grumble. I don't want to fight him today. I just want him gone.

"Whatever?" Before I can react, he backhands me hard enough to knock me flat on my bed. "You best learn manners, boy." He keeps one hand on my chest and slaps me again, harder this time. And it's then I can smell the alcohol on his breath. Of course he's drunk.

"Get the fuck off me!" I shove him back as hard as I can. He stumbles.

"Xavier! You ready for this history test, man?" Brant, my cousin and best friend, says from my bedroom door. He's walked in on my dad and I fighting more than once. Somehow, he always knows how to end it with just words.

My father lets out a low rumble of a growl and leaves the room with the remnants of the letter still in his hand. I lean up on my elbows and watch him leave with fire in my eyes and ice in my veins. One day, I swear to fuck I'll pay him back. For now, I'm just biding my damn time.

I sit up slowly and touch my cheek and lip with hardly a wince. "Motherfucker is going to get what's coming to him one day."

Brant chuckles as he closes my bedroom door. "What was it about this time?"

"Acceptance letter to Ohio State or some shit."

He raises an eyebrow as he sits at my desk. "I thought you chose Brystone."

"I did. I already sent them a promise letter. It's confirmed and everything. The coach and administration understand my situation and are happy to call me when they have paperwork. I just drive out there and take care of it."

Brant nods. "Good. I can't wait until we're all there. All of us back on one team. We're gonna miss you next year, man."

This makes me smile. I shrug. "Awe. You'll be okay. You're just as good as I am. And you know I'll put in a good word for you. Coach is already working on a recruitment package for you, Sterling, Kody, and Drake."

Brant, Sterling, Kody, and Drake are all my cousins. My dad has a couple of brothers and a sister. I grew up with their kids. We're all as close as siblings. We also have another cousin, Dylan. We're close to her, maybe even more than to each other, but Dylan's dad is extremely overprotective. He rarely lets her do anything. I'm surprised he let her be a cheerleader. I have a sneaking suspicion it's because we're all on the football team. He knows we'll keep her safe.

I can't really blame the guy. He's nice enough, but he's a State Senator. He gets a lot of fucking attention, and Dylan often catches the brunt of decisions he makes. We've had to step in more times than we can count when other students in school start harassing her for her father's decisions. Dylan takes it all like a goddamn Warrior Princess, though. She never lets any of it get to her.

"Ready to head out? Onyx is waiting. Everyone is already there."

I glance at my clock. It's nearly nine. "Huh. Fucker must have been fucking some bitch behind headquarters again. He's usually home before now."

Brant chuckles. "Unless he's getting his rocks off. Think he's passed out yet?"

"Maybe. He was already swaying when he got up here. The hit wasn't even that strong. I don't think he left a mark on me."

Brant looks over my face. "Just a little red under your eye. Not noticeable."

I stand and glance in the mirror on my door quickly as I grab my belt. "I wonder how many drinks he had before he got home if he was drunk enough to not leave a mark this time." I put my belt on and quickly change into a black t-shirt. I run my fingers through my hair, giving myself the perfect messy look.

"Well, however many it was, it's too bad he didn't crash into a tree on his way home. Do you think your mom is out yet?"

I chuckle. "She mixed her Xanax with Prince Valium long ago. She's out."

"Then let's get the hell out of here. I need a beer. My dad's new wife is driving me fucking crazy."

I laugh. "Driving you crazy by how nice she is? Or how your dick reacts to her?"

He grins and shoves me out of the bedroom door when I open it. "Asshole," he whispers.

We sneak quietly past my parent's bedroom. It's partially ajar, so I peek inside. My dad is sprawled facedown on the bed with his pants still on. No shirt. My mom, just as I predicted, is dead to the world. Neither of them will be moving for the rest of the night.

I chuckle when I see mom's open Valium container on dad's nightstand as I step away from the door. "We could drop a bomb on the house. They wouldn't wake up. He took one of her pills again."

Brant rolls his eyes. "I seriously wonder sometimes if your dad has a drug problem. Like he just goes into the evidence room and takes bricks of cocaine."

I laugh as we walk down the stairs. "Nah. It would be the prescription drugs he'd be into. He loves knocking his ass out with mom's shit. I'm not sure how his drinking and pill taking doesn't affect his job." I lead Brant out the front door.

"Want me to drive?" he asks. "I took my dad's Corvette."

I grin. "His pride and joy."

Brant laughs. "I'm his pride and joy. The car is just a nice perk."

I shake my head as I head for the garage. "I'll drive myself. Might get lucky tonight."

"You *need* to get your dick sucked. You've been quite the asshole on the field."

I laugh and wink over my shoulder. "Maybe I'll get some guy to loosen me up."

Brant laughs as he ducks in his dad's car and takes off. I jump in my Camaro and follow him to our club. We like it so much because the owner doesn't have a problem serving us. We've always thought it had a little to do with the fact that Dylan has enough money to pay him off. She doesn't get to come out with us all the time, but when she does, she always

8

has the bartender grab the owner before she sits down. They talk for a few moments, and then he walks away while she comes to us.

However it happens, we aren't complaining. She has more than enough money to slip the guy a few thousand to keep quiet. And she'd tell us if he started making any demands she couldn't handle or didn't want to take part in. She knows we'd deal with it.

After a twenty minute drive, we pull into Onyx and park. It looks a lot busier than usual. The line is even still long. Thank God we have connections. We step out of our cars and walk to the bouncer at the front of the line. He lets us right in, despite the grumbles of those in the crowd. We don't get carded or anything.

When we get in, I immediately spot our group. Dylan looks a little distant and upset. Sterling, Drake, and Kody all surround her in our favorite corner booth in the VIP section of the club. We like that we can overlook everything in the club but can't be bothered by people we don't want anything to do with.

A perk of being royalty, to an extent, at our high school is the unlimited admiration and attention we get. It's also one of the downfalls. We always have people sucking up to us and wanting to be a part of our group. While we can basically do and get away with anything we want, our status is coveted by others. It's more an annoyance to me than it is flattery. I'm sure there are a couple in my group who would disagree, though.

Brant and I make our way to our group. I catch the eye of the server in our section. I don't need to say anything. She knows our order. It's a perk I don't mind. I slide in next to Sterling. Brant sits on the other side next to Drake.

"Dylan's asshole biology teacher failed her," Sterling says.

I shake my head and look at her with a raised eyebrow. "What? Why?"

She sniffles and shrugs. "I wouldn't dissect the pig fetus. It made me sick. And not just the smell of formaldehyde. I just couldn't do it. He said if I didn't, he'd fail me. So I walked out of class. He berated me the whole time. Told me some just aren't cut out for doing what it takes. Some of the other students agreed. I heard one of them say that I get special treatment because of who my father is."

"That's bullshit," I growl low. "He can't fail you for that."

She looks at me with watery eyes. "There were other girls in the class who didn't have to. One said it was religious reasons, but I think it's because she sucked his dick or fucked him or something."

"Wouldn't be surprised." I take a long swallow of the cold, light beer in my glass. Dark has always tasted like shit to me. Too strong. Not enough taste. I'll take a Coors over an ale any day of the week.

"What are we going to do about this?" Drake asks. "We can't let him fail her. She'll get kicked off the cheerleading squad."

I shrug. I'm the leader on and off the field with my group. "Simple. We use our advantage while systematically destroying the fucker."

Kody grins. "How're we going to destroy him? I'm game. I hate that guy."

"We use her dad. I know you don't like whining to him and being daddy's little girl, but do it in this case," I respond. "As for him? We'll set up Go Pros in the room. We'll catch him doing something we can use against him."

Dylan smiles a little. "Thank you, Xavier. I don't know why I've been so upset about it. I knew you guys would take care of it."

Sterling chuckles. "Not like you wouldn't have figured out some way to get him back. You're not at all innocent."

Dylan laughs. "Only when I get pissed off enough."

I smile as we all start loosening up. One thing I can say for us. Though we may be close and basically the Kings and Queen of our school, we aren't assholes. Not unless we have to be. We don't go around bullying anyone. We all work hard. We're admired. People want to be us. But we certainly don't strike the fear of God into anyone. No one fucks with us, though, because everyone knows we don't and won't take shit from anyone.

I can't wait until we all head off to college and get to be on our own. The only one who won't be with us is Dylan. She has dreams. Big, big dreams. She loves being a cheerleader, but she wants to be a chef and own her own restaurant. She plans on going to some fancy university in Chicago. We'll miss the hell out of her, but no way we won't visit her. She'll do the same.

After a couple of hours, we're all feeling pretty good. But the mood quickly sours when I see a few people from our school at a table near us snorting some white powder off the table they're sitting at. We might drink, but we draw the line at that shit.

"That's fucking brazen," Sterling says quietly.

"No shit," I murmur back.

One of them recognizes us and stands. "Hey, ya'll. Wanna take a few hits with us?" he asks when he reaches our table. "Guaranteed to make your night a blast." He laughs as he hands us a small baggie.

"Are you fucking insane?" I growl, slapping his hand away from us. "Get that shit out of here."

"Come on. Don't be like that, dude. Just trying to share the good time." He actually pouts.

"We aren't interested in you or your brand of fun. Walk away," Kody growls dangerously.

No sooner do the words come out of his mouth, I hear shouts. I glance towards the dance floor and see people running and screaming. They run for exits, but a lot of people in black uniforms that say 'Police' across the chest are converging on them from the very doors they're trying to run out. I usually have inside information of when the cops are planning a raid anywhere in the city. So does Brant. I have no idea why I didn't know about this one.

I don't have time to ponder, though, because we all need to get the hell out of here. I don't want to be caught in a bust with alcohol in my system. I sure as hell don't want anyone at this table to either. I'm the only one who's eighteen. Everyone else here is sixteen or seventeen.

I get up quickly and spring into action. We all duck down as we run behind the bar. Another good thing about whatever Dylan does to make the owner like us is that we know where a lot of escapes are that others don't. Except maybe employees. If we need to make a quick exit and not be seen, we can.

It's happened before. A few of us have had girls all over us who wouldn't give it up. We've used the secret exits to escape without causing a scene. Dylan has had a few guys who wouldn't leave her alone, even after warnings from us. After we've gotten her out, we've taken care of them. They've never bothered her again, but we're grateful for the ability to get her out quietly.

I make sure everyone else gets to the door. Not seeing any cops, I start pushing them all towards it. "Go!" I whisper yell. Dylan looks up at me with terrified eyes. "Go, Dylan! Get out of here!"

"What about you?" she cries.

"I'll be fine! Go! I need to find Brant!"

Brant is the only one who wasn't with us when the raid started. He'd just gone to the bathroom not long before. I duck out of view of the police, but I'm not really sure I'd need to. They all seem pretty occupied with the numerous people in the club on the dancefloor, many of whom are fighting with them.

So, I run towards the bathrooms, praying no one pays me any attention. Hopefully, these guys are as stupid as my father is. He's had his ass saved more than once by one of his partners because he's not observant in the slightest. I'm sure it's because he drinks on the job.

I let out a breath when I reach the bathrooms. They must have checked this hall already because there's no one in it. I duck into the bathroom and look around. There's a window open and no one in any of the stalls.

"Fuck, I hope to hell you got out of here," I whisper.

Not wanting to chance going back out the door, I climb up on a urinal and out the window. I grunt a little because it's not that large. I have to squeeze myself out of it. It's a good thing I chose to go feet first because the ground below would be a hard fall. It's only a few feet down this way. I let go of the window and land in a crouch.

"Nice landing, kid," a deep voice that sends shivers down my spine says from the shadows behind me. "I was wondering how many people would dare come out that window after I saw the first one do it and take off. Didn't catch him, but I've caught six."

Holy fuck, I hope to hell Brant wasn't one of them. I stand slowly as I let out a breath. I'm the son of a cop. One thing I've learned is to not make sudden movements. So, when I turn, I do it just as deliberately as I had when I stood.

I expected a cocky fucker. Most cops I know are. I didn't expect the tall, dark, sexy drink of water standing in front of me with piercing blue eyes I could drown in and die happy. I didn't expect his sinful glare to go straight to my cock.

I swallow. Hard. It does nothing to quench my sudden thirst for this man, though. I'm usually the one who commands the boys I'm with in the bedroom. Only those close to me know that secret. The boys I've been with wouldn't dare tell a soul. I have a reputation to protect.

Boys. That's just what they are compared to the person standing in front of me right now. They are all boys. All of them. They may be my age, but they are nothing compared to him.

Fuck.

I'd drop to my knees and do whatever this guy asked me to. I bet he could bring me the kind of pleasure I've longed for but never quite accomplished. I highly doubt I'd have to guide him into position. He'd just know.

I mentally shake myself out of my fantasy. First of all, I doubt he's gay. If he is, I'm far too young for a man like him. Not that I'd care. I'd fall at his feet and kiss the ground he walked on if he asked me to. Second, he's a cop. Who is about to arrest me. And third, there's no way I can flirt my way out of this one. He doesn't look like the type who would fall for it.

"Don't suppose I can talk you into not telling my father about this," I say, hoping I'll at least get that much out of him. "It would just make things worse for me."

He raises an eyebrow. "Do I look like the type of guy who gives a fuck who your daddy is and how bad it would be for you?"

I shrug. "Nope. But you're a cop. So is he. If I told you he'd probably beat the shit out of me for this, you'd care because it's your job."

"Is he going to beat the shit out of you? Or is that just your way of getting on my good side so I don't tell daddy his precious son is fucking around at a drug party?"

I chuckle and nod. "Fair enough. It's the truth, but I can handle him. What if I said I was eighteen?"

He shrugs but doesn't move from his spot against the wall of the club. "Then daddy wouldn't have to know. It'd be up to you to tell him so he can come bail your ass out. Turn around."

I have half a mind to run, but I don't doubt he'd be able to keep up. So, I let out a sigh and turn around. When I feel the cold metal of the cuffs hit my wrists, I know it's over for me. I can not only kiss my place on the football team goodbye, but I can also kiss my scholarship goodbye. My entire college career. I'm not even certain I care too much about any of that. Right now, all I can think about is my cousins and wonder if they got out.

And the tingles this cop's hands are shooting through my entire body as he leads me to his squad.

Chapter Two

☪ Colton ☪

I glance in the rearview mirror at the kid I arrested not long ago at the Onyx. Something about him is pulling at places it shouldn't be. Like my heart. And my fucking dick. He's truly gorgeous. Maybe the most handsome guy I've ever seen. The first one to make me feel anything at all for a very long time.

But he's quiet.

Too quiet.

Xavier Remington hasn't looked up at me since I put him in the car. He's in the backseat looking down at his feet with his legs spread apart to make himself more comfortable. He's tall, and the back seat of a squad car is made to be uncomfortable. Even more so for big guys like me or him.

"Tell me what you were doing at that club," I say after a few more moments of silence. Anything to get him talking again. Something about him makes me want to know everything. Especially what he was doing in a club like Onyx.

He shrugs but doesn't look up. "Don't you have to read me my rights or something? You know. Right to remain silent. Right to not talk to

15

you. Right to an attorney. And then ask me if I'm smart enough to understand what you said. Then if I wish to talk to you."

I can't help the smile that spreads across my face. I chuckle. "Sounds like you already know them."

"My dad's a cop. Remember? They've been ingrained in me ever since I was born."

I chuckle again. "Who's your dad?"

"Buckley Remington. Ace detective extraordinaire," he answers. So much sarcasm laces his voice, though, it makes me raise an eyebrow. "You might have heard him with his whore behind the station," he says low enough I'm sure he doesn't think I can hear.

There are a couple of Remington's who work at the department. I thought he was just being a smartass when he said his dad might beat him. Now, I'm not so sure. Buckley Remington is quite the asshole. I know he has a drinking problem. But he's the higher-up's pet. Getting them to do shit about it is like hitting a target dead center with a Glock from three hundreds yards away. If that sounds impossible, it's because it damn well is.

It's also a well-known fact that Buckley Remington likes his girls young. His current fling is one of our newest officers. She's barely twenty-one. She's also not the only one he fucks around with. I'm sure he thinks none of us know, but he's a frequent shopper in our very own red-light district. Most of the time, he's on duty when he goes there. Fucker is his own brand of tool.

I clear my throat. "Your dad isn't all that well-liked around the department."

He lets out something between a chuckle and a grunt. "Nope. He's not all that well-liked anywhere. Except with the command staff. Probably gives them dick or something."

I'm quiet a few moments as I think. Something about all of this just doesn't sit right with me. "So, why were you at a club known for drugs?"

He shifts a little and slumps down in his seat as he leans his head back against the headrest and closes his eyes. "We don't go there for the drugs. We aren't into that shit. We know it happens. We know the owner is lax. We go because he serves us alcohol. It's a nice little reprieve when the day is fucked up. You know. Like, when your mom tells you everyday how

16

much you've fucked up her life. Or your dad tries to punch you but only slaps you because he's too fucking drunk to know the difference. Then screams at you about going to the college he's picked for you because your life and choices don't fucking matter."

Now we're getting somewhere. "So, he hit you because you decided you don't want to go to the college he's chosen."

He shrugs, but those silver eyes that mesmerize me stay closed. Probably for the best. What they do to me is probably a crime around the world. "Doesn't matter. I don't need him to pay for college. He knows it. I have my pick of any college in the country. And I'm good enough to get a full scholarship. I only need him until I pack up and leave after I graduate." He opens his eyes then and chuckles. "Ironic, huh? This fuck up will actually be the one that ruins it all."

I keep my eyes on the road because if I look back at him again, I can't be responsible for my actions. He looks so fucking upset that all I want to do is take him in my arms and kiss it all away. I mentally slap myself for the damn thought.

"You went to the club to drink. No drugs. None of that shit."

"Nope. But again. Doesn't matter now, does it? You may as well just put me in a cell and throw away the key because as soon as my dad finds out, he'll kick me out. I could probably stay with a cousin, but my life as I know it is over because no college would accept me with a drinking charge on my record. They expect their quarterbacks to be clean. Lead by example. Probably for the best, right? Maybe this is my wake-up call. Can't be a badass and a good kid. Eventually, the tightrope is going to break. Lines I toe will eventually be crossed."

I glance down at the computer screen all squads are equipped with. His address isn't too far away from here, so I make an executive decision and turn left towards his house instead of continuing to Headquarters. A block away from his house, I pull over and stop. He'd closed his eyes again. When we stop, he doesn't move.

I sigh and cut the lights and engine. "Promise me that all you were doing at that club is drinking. That you weren't into the drugs. You're not selling. You aren't part of the illegal underground weapons market I'm positive he has going on." I lean back in my seat and glance at him over my shoulder. He's watching me with wide eyes and a slightly open mouth.

I can see how shocked he is, but all I really want to do is plunge my tongue into his mouth just to see how he tastes.

Fuck. What the hell is wrong with me?

I don't even really know why I told him about the drugs and weapons trade. This case is supposed to be top secret. No one knows I'm working it except the Chief of the department. My taskforce, while large, are all cops from other areas that I've pulled in because I suspect that there are some cops in my own department that are a part of what's going on. It's the only way it can stay as secret as it has for so long.

"All I was doing was drinking," he finally says to me after staring at me for a good while.

I nod but say nothing. I get out of the car and make my way to the backdoor. I open it to let him out. He watches me cautiously and confused but eventually slides out. He stands in front of me curiously as I take his arm. I turn him around and unlock the cuffs.

"Who were the friends you were with?" I swallow because touching his skin makes me inadvertently shiver. I let him go.

He turns around slowly and rubs his wrists as he watches me with furrowed brows. "My cousins. Sterling, Dylan, Kody, Brant, and Drake."

I nod and slide back into my driver's seat. I feel his eyes on me. When I glance back, Xavier looks away quickly, but knowing that he was watching me as I was sitting down does things to me I know it shouldn't.

I try to focus on anything else other than him and my reaction. I look up the notes from other officers involved in the raid to see if any of the names he gave me show up. They don't. I don't know why I feel relieved to see that, but I am.

"It looks like they all got away, but I'll keep an eye out."

I can feel his eyes still on me. They send delightful shivers down my spine. For the thousandth time in I don't even know how long anymore, I quietly berate myself. My reaction is illogical. He's eighteen. Legal. But he's in high school. Doubtful he's gay. Not like many around here know I am. Just the failed relationships I've left in my wake. I'm not going to waste my time or anyone else's if I don't feel a connection, though.

Like the connection I have with him.

Jesus. What the fuck is wrong with me? He's twenty years younger. I could be his fucking father. I know I need to get a grip. Maybe it's just been too long since I've actually had good sex with anyone other than my hand. I need to go home and release the tension. Maybe then I'll stop thinking very inappropriate thoughts about this young man.

I close my eyes for a moment as I close my screen. I make a mental note to check on his friends later, though I really shouldn't. They were in the club. They were all drinking. They should all, at the very least, get cited for that alone. Instead, I tell myself that they aren't who I was after. They don't deserve to go down in a bust related to drugs if they weren't doing it.

How do I know they weren't? Well, I believe Xavier. I can tell he was drinking, but I've seen far drunker men over the course of my career. I doubt he's had more than a couple. His eyes are still clear. He's not exhibiting any signs of drug use. No. He's not my target. And I believe if he's not taking part in the drug activity, it's unlikely that his friends are. I've been around long enough to know at least a few things.

I take a breath as I get out of my car. "You're free to go."

He gives me a bewildered look that makes him look even more handsome. I try to stop the low groan before it escapes my mouth, but it doesn't work. This is ridiculous. Whatever is happening right now is completely wrong.

Xavier looks at me. "Why are you doing this? You should just take me to jail. Book me. My dad will see the paperwork without me even saying a word to him. He'll get his way. No other college will take me, but he'll pull some strings with Texas A&M. I'll be forced to go there."

I lean against my car and cross my arms over my chest. "You want me to be honest?"

He shrugs. "Yeah."

I look up at the sky before looking straight ahead at the house in front of me. "I don't know. The cop in me wants me to arrest you. Book you for a lot of charges. Fleeing the police. Drinking underage. Drug use. You were in the club. Logic would say you were using. Tests would come back saying you didn't." I shrug. "But that isn't the part of me I'm listening to." I look at him. "I'm giving you a huge break here. You understand that, don't you?"

He nods slowly, still a little confused as to what the hell I'm doing. Fuck, so am I. "Yeah. I get it."

"Don't let me down, Xavier. I mean it." I reach for my wallet and take out one of my business cards. I hand it to him. "Office phone is on the front. Cell is on the back. Call day or night if you need anything."

He looks down at the card. "Colton DeLise. Detective." He looks back at me. "You work with my dad and uncle."

I nod. "I do. Maybe it's why I decided to keep your name out of things." I'm lying. The truth is, I can't bring myself to ruin his life. I know this will. Even a drinking charge will fuck him over. That's not even factoring in his dick of a father. "Do we need to go back and get your car?"

He shakes his head with a small smile as he takes out his own wallet. I don't know why it pleases me to see him put my card in it and not toss it on the ground. His eyes meet mine again. Fuck if I don't let myself drown in their depths.

"Nah. One of my cousins would have grabbed it." He grins.

I chuckle. "Good to have a team you can trust on your side."

"We're all pretty close." He shuffles his feet and leans against my car next to me.

It's my turn to give him a confused glance. I figured he would have run home by now. Not be hesitantly leaning against my car like he's testing me to see if I'll tell him to get the fuck home or let him stay and talk to me.

He turns and puts his arms on the roof of my car. He rests his chin on them. I try to stop myself from noticing that tight black shirt of his that leaves nothing to the imagination slide up a little. I can see a hint of his back, but that's not what draws my attention. It's how muscular he looks. His jeans rest low enough on his hips that I can see the edge of the V-shape leading underneath his waistband. Because that's not going to drive me crazy later. It's driving me fucking insane right now.

"I'm a straight A student," he says after he stands next to me for a while. "He still manages to tell me it's not good enough." He chuckles. "But that doesn't really bother me. It's the team. I'm an All-Star quarterback. I work my ass off. Even during the off season. I stay in shape. I even do a lot of charity shit. It's not good enough for him, though. It used to be. But then he started drinking. The older I get, the worse he gets. He finds things to nitpick. School is just the latest thing."

I don't know why he's telling me all of this, but I don't care. I like his deep, velvety voice. I breathe in a deep breath and take a chance to feel

20

him out. "When I came out to my dad, he very promptly kicked me out. I was sixteen. Lived on the streets a bit. A teacher I liked took me in. I still consider her and her husband more parental units to me than my biological ones. Haven't spoken to my dad since."

He looks at me. Finally. I can't get enough of his silver eyes. I hope I'm not misreading the fire in them as he looks at me. "What about your mom?"

I chuckle. "Couldn't tell you. She left when I was pretty young. I haven't given much of a shit to track her down. Last I knew, she lived with some drug dealer in Montana."

He makes a face and looks away again. I inwardly whimper at the loss. Fucking pathetic of me. "My mom enjoys her Xanax and Valium. It's her escape from my dad. She hates him touching her. Knocks her ass out until late morning. She also loves blaming me for how her life has turned out. If it weren't for me, she would've left. Shit like that. It throws me into a depression that they both just tell me is a phase. I'll be okay." He shrugs. "Probably will when I'm out from under them."

We fall quiet once more. The nice thing about Brystone Springs is that it's small enough to still be able to see the stars in the Texas sky and hear the crickets chirp at night while being large enough to not feel stifling. I sigh quietly because I can't help but feel a little bit disappointed that he didn't react slightly more to my admission of being gay. I shouldn't fucking care. Dammit. I do, though. Maybe I can feel him out more. Would brushing his hand be crossing a line?

"Listen, uh…" I run my fingers through my hair as I stand. If I lean next to him anymore, I'm going to do something stupid. Like kiss him. He's intoxicating. Something about his scent. It's fresh, yet spicy. Unique. I let out a breath and turn to him. He's watching me over his shoulder. "Don't let anyone know about this. Okay? If they find out about me letting you go and erasing anything to do with your group, I could get fired."

He turns and leans against my car as he nods. "I won't. I know you're putting your ass on the line here. Don't really know why, though."

I smile and chuckle. "Because I think you were in the wrong place at the wrong time. I don't think this is something to fuck up your life over. I certainly don't want to be the one who ends your future before it even starts." I shrug with a half smile. "And maybe I'm secretly hoping you'll come to me before you go out and do something stupid again. Like drink after getting into it with your dad."

He gives me a smile I'm sure melts the panties off any woman he gives it to. It certainly makes mine feel like they're on fire. "Playing the hero here, detective?"

I laugh. "Maybe a little. Complex of being a cop, you know. Always gotta be the hero of the story."

He smiles as he looks down. He looks back up at me after a few moments. "You're a lot different than I thought. You're not as… I don't know. Hard."

"I'm still hard, all right." At least my dick is. "But I'm not a complete asshole. Just… don't… let me catch you in a place like that again. This will probably go in one ear and out the other, but there's a lot of shit going on in this town. This case just landed on my desk a little while ago. Since then, the floodgates have opened. I've found a lot of things out that… well, they're dangerous. I don't want to see you go down for something you're not involved in."

He nods. "Sure thing, detective." He glances towards the direction of his house. "I should probably head home. Not like I'm worried about them waking up, but I do have a test tomorrow." He looks down as he pushes off my car.

I wish I could keep him here all night, but I know that's selfish of me. "Probably a good idea to get home then."

He doesn't move, though. I realize he's waiting for me to get back into my car. The gesture makes me chuckle, but it makes me feel a little warm inside that he wants to wait for me to get into my car before he leaves.

So, I do what he silently asks me to. I slide into the driver's seat of my squad. I don't miss the way he watches me do it. Or that he licks his lips when I look back up at him in surprise. But I don't have time to formulate the words my head wants me to before he walks away.

"Goodnight, Detective Sweet Ass."

I blink a few times as if I'm coming out of a stupor and watch him walk down the middle of the street towards his house with his hands in his pockets. A few moments later I force myself to breathe. Apparently, I forgot how.

Holy hell, that did not just happen. It was a figment of my obviously sex-deprived imagination. I need to go home. I need to take a shower and rub one out. When morning comes around I'm positive all of the so far out of line thoughts I'm having will be gone. He didn't just watch me like he was wondering what it would be like on his knees for me.

As I drive away, I know deep down I'm never going to be able to get those eyes out of my head. The way they looked like melting silver when he looked at me. I don't even need to think about it any longer to know just how fucked I am.

Chapter Three

☪ Xavier ☪

(One Week Later)

"You okay?" Brant asks when I saunter off the field after throwing my second interception of the game.

I throw my helmet on the ground and rub my eyes with a low growl. "Fuck!" I rest my elbows on my knees and drop my head in my hands. "This is the worst game I've ever played. And that counts the one where I played with bruised ribs and could barely breathe."

"What do you want me to do, Remington?" Coach asks as he sits next to me. "Halftime is coming up. You want to take the time to get your head back in the damn game? Or do you want me to throw Brant in there?"

I don't hesitate. I've learned a thing or two over the past couple of years. When to let my backup lead is one of them. I take off my Captain's armband. "Put Brant in. I'm off today. I don't know why." I hand Brant my armband.

He takes it and puts it on, then pats my back. "I got you. I'll bring us back." He jumps up and jogs over to the edge of the field to warm up.

"How pissed is your dad gonna be?" Coach asks.

I shrug and keep my eyes on the field. "Fuck if I know. Don't really care. I'll be out of there soon enough."

"Well, heads up. He's walking this way. Want me to stick around?"

"No." I shake my head and nod to the field. "Team needs you."

He pats my back and stands. He walks towards his assistant. I can't help but smile a little because he's closer than he normally would be. I know he's within earshot in case shit goes down with my dad. It wouldn't be the first time. I'm sure it won't be the last.

My father sits down next to me on the bench and sighs. "What the fuck, Xavier? Where's your head? I don't think you've ever thrown two interceptions in a game."

I don't look at him. "Not feeling good, dad. It's hot. I'm probably thirsty or something."

"Well, get your damn head in the game. Fuck. You're embarrassing me. I talk you up at work all the damn time. I finally get some of my colleagues to come watch my boy play, and this is what you give them? This piss poor performance? This isn't your level. You're playing like a fucking rookie."

I shrug and stand. "Don't worry. I won't be embarrassing you anymore today, pops. Brant is taking over."

I walk away before he can say a word and smile as Coach intercepts him before he can follow me. I beeline for the locker room and lock myself in Coach's office after stopping by my locker and grabbing my gym bag. It's the one place my father not only won't think to look, but couldn't see me in even if he tried. The windows are blacked out and have a black curtain. No one is seeing me in here.

I start taking off my gear. I know exactly what my problem is. It's not my dad. It's not that the team we're playing is just that good. They aren't. My problem is that it's been a week since the raid on the club. A week since we enacted our plan on Dylan's teacher.

And since meeting that sexy as fuck detective. I can't get those eyes out of my head. I can't get him out of my head. The way he filled out those damn jeans and protective vest. How his ass looked as he got into his squad. I've gotten off an embarrassing number of times to images of his face. I've almost texted him just to talk but stopped myself because I don't

25

want to come off as desperate. Though, I'm fucking desperate to see him again.

Not that I feel crazy or anything. I roll my eyes and shake my head. It's definitely insane to be thinking about a guy I know nothing about the way I have been. Especially since he's probably old enough to be my father. I'm sure if I said anything to him about the fantasies he has rolling through my head, he'd probably tell me I have a daddy complex or some shit.

I mentally punch myself and head for the showers to quickly wash the sweat and dirt off me. Hot detective isn't the only thing on my mind. While he's troubling me, he's definitely not the reason I can't fucking concentrate on completing a pass.

Nope.

What's really pissing me off is what we saw on our GoPro cameras. That son of a bitch has a whole group of girls he's getting blowjobs from before classes start. One of them, who Dylan says is a star pupil, fucks him right there on his desk almost every damn day.

Nothing about most of it looks nonconsensual. The girls often start the whole fucking thing. It's bad enough that they're all cheerleaders and all talk shit about Dylan just before the whole sexual encounter starts. I could easily ruin the little bitches. I still might.

The part that makes my stomach churn is what I saw on the cameras this morning. One of the cheerleaders he had giving him a blowjob is barely sixteen fucking years old. She's new to the school and has only just joined the team. The look on her face was pure terror. I don't know what the fucker said to her that our cameras didn't catch, but she definitely didn't want to be sucking his old man dick.

She hasn't been at the school long enough for it to be going on for long, but I hate the fact that she didn't come to us. She knows that when it comes to what goes on at this school, we have a lot of pull and clout. Everyone knows that. It's unlikely teachers even fuck with us. What's happening with Dylan is so rare it makes me think there's more shit going down that I'm not aware of. I don't like it.

And that all brings me back to Detective Sexy. I finish my shower and grab my towel. The team should be coming in soon, so I quickly dry off on my way back to the office. I start getting dressed and glance at my phone. This is something the police need to be involved in, but his words about shit happening keeps coming back to me. He got cops from other areas to help him with the case he's working on because he can't trust those within the department. I didn't recognize any of the ones I saw at Onyx.

I've been going back and forth on if I do or don't want to pull him into this. I could just report it to the School Resource Officer. I could make a copy of the video and give him one of the copies. The issue is given what Colton said, I don't know who to trust and who not to. I don't know if anything would get done if I gave it to our SRO.

I grab my phone and leave my gear and gym bag in here. The team should be getting off the field for halftime right now. I sit down on a bench and wait for them as I make my decision. I need to text Colton. I pull up his number that I saved into my phone the very night he gave me his card and send him a text.

Xavier: Hey, Detective. It's Xavier. We met last week. You said if I needed anything to contact you. Well, the time has come, and it's important. I have a game today. I'm not playing, but I'm at the high school. Can you meet me? Text me when you're here.

I let out a breath and put my phone down as the team starts coming in. They're cheering and high-fiving each other, so I assume Brant is doing good at pulling them out of the fucking gutter I led them into. I smile because my cousin is just as good out there as I am. We've worked our whole lives to be the best. The only reason he's not the starting quarterback is because I haven't graduated yet. As soon as I do, Brant will be out there kicking ass each week like I do now.

For now, he's one of our running backs. He doesn't play all the time, just when he's needed, but he's just as good at that as being quarterback. Thankfully, we didn't need him out there playing running back today. He was fresh and ready to go in for me.

"Yeah! Nice throw! I wasn't sure I was going to catch it, but fuck! Dude! Right in my hands! That was like a move right out of Xavier's playbook!" Sterling exclaims as the team seemingly dance into the locker room.

I grin. "I'm sorry I missed it."

"Man, it was incredible!" Drake says as a smiling Brant sits next to me.

"Got us on the board, at least." Brant's eyes twinkle, and I can't help but be proud as hell.

I grin and high-five him. "Nice job!"

"Alright, guys," Coach says as he walks in and stands in the middle of us. His eyes meet mine. "I was going to ask if you wanted to come out after halftime. Looks like you made your decision."

I nod. "Not in the right frame of mind, Coach. Brant has the team. I'll cheer from the sidelines. The team needs someone who can fully focus on the game. I can't. I have some shit that needs to be dealt with. I'll be good next game."

"Okay," Coach says. "It's your team. Your decision." He turns back to the team. "I don't think I need to say much here. We're down by fourteen, but I know we can get it back. Keep playing like you just were. Trust your Quarterback. Keep your eyes on the ball. Adjust out there. Play smart. Defensive line. You're missing blocks out there. Morale was down a bit. But we're on the scoreboard. This game isn't that important, but an undefeated team getting their asses handed to them by a team that hasn't won a game isn't something I want to see. Offense. Remington wasn't the only issue out there. He missed a few passes, threw a couple interceptions, but you guys need to get open. This can't ride on one man's shoulders. Now rehydrate. Catch your breath. Do what you gotta do to right your minds. Let's show this city why the hell we're number one and deserve that championship trophy we're battling towards!"

I smile as the team lets out a resounding cheer. As they all go about their halftime rituals. I turn to Brant. "Nice job out there. Team is fired up."

He grins before sobering quickly. "Did you figure out what we're gonna do about the teacher? I know that's why you're off today."

I sigh and nod. "Yeah. Remember the detective I told you about?"

He smiles again. "The one who knocked the great Xavier Remington on his ass? Nope. Don't remember him."

I laugh and playfully shove him. "Asshole. Anyway. I texted him. Asked him to meet me here. I'll turn it over to him, but I need to talk to Rosie. She needs to be prepared for the shitstorm about to come down."

Brant nods. "You do that. I saw her sniffling and walking towards the parking lot. Pretty sure she probably didn't wanna be near the girls. Dylan went with her."

"Good." I stand and grab my phone. "Meet you back out there."

Brant grins and joins the team to boost their morale even more. He's learned very well. It makes me feel good about leaving the team to him. I know he'll make them proud. But most of all, I know he'll make himself proud.

I make my way out to the parking lot and look for Dylan and Rosie. It doesn't take me long to spot them. Rosie is sitting on the grass in the shade near the building in tears. Dylan is wrapped around her, rocking her back and forth. When I reach them, I kneel down and raise an eyebrow.

"He's at the game," Dylan whispers.

Rosie, not knowing I'm in front of her, lets out a squeak and wipes her eyes vigorously as her head snaps to me. "Xavier!"

"I haven't told her," Dylan mouths to me.

I nod. "Hey, Rosie. You okay?"

She nods with wide eyes. She looks frantically at Dylan before she looks back at me. "I'm okay! I just… had a hard day." She smiles, but I can see it's faked. "Why aren't you in uniform?"

"Brant took over." I pause for a moment. "Rosie, uh…" I take a breath and run my fingers through my still damp hair. "Why didn't you come to one of us? You know if anything is going on with you, we'll help you. Me. Drake. Brant. Sterling. Kody. Hell, even Dylan."

She bites her lip and looks at Dylan again. Dylan smiles softly and runs her fingers through Rosie's disheveled hair. With the tears she'd been crying ruining her make-up, I can see the bags under her eyes. We pulled the footage just before school, but this happened last night. There's no doubt in my mind that she didn't sleep even a second.

"How long has he been forcing you?" Dylan whispers as she hugs her.

Rosie bursts into tears and curls into herself. Dylan looks up when she hears the crowd start roaring with cheers. The teams are running back on the field. She looks at me. She's so obviously torn. She wants to stay with her friend, but she also knows she needs to cover for her.

I jerk my head towards the field as I take Rosie in my arms and hug her tightly while she sobs so hard, my heart feels like it's breaking. "Go. Cover for her."

Dylan nods as she stands. "Okay."

"All the other girls told me that it's what they do," she whispers after several minutes. "That I have to. Or I'll fail his class. I'm already struggling. I don't understand it. He makes me feel so stupid." She hiccups as she grips my shirt. "He writes comments on my tests. Things like asking me how I could miss such a simple question. And he says things from that movie with Tom Hanks. 'Stupid is as stupid does.' He keeps me after class and berates me while he looks me over. It makes me feel so gross."

"Rosie, we told you that if you ever needed anything to come to us," I whisper as I rub my hand up and down her back.

"They said Dylan did it, too." She sniffles. "I shouldn't have believed them."

"Oh, honey. She doesn't. They're lying. Don't blame yourself. How long has this been happening?"

She sniffles again as I sway gently with her. "Last night he made me suck him off. A w-week ago h-he…" She trails off, unable to finish. She doesn't need to. I can tell by her sobs what the sick fucker did to her.

All I can do is hug her tighter because I don't want to tell her again that she should have come to us. It'll only make her feel like she fucked up and could've stopped it. The truth is, she could've. We would have helped her. But none of what happened to her is her fault. None of it.

"Do you trust me?" I ask her.

She nods. "I trust Dylan. And she trusts you and the guys."

"Then you trust that I'll get this dealt with, but I need your help."

She sniffles and nods again. "I trust you."

"I only have what happened last night on my video. We could have just used the shit from before, but it all looked consensual. Last night was the first time we saw something that will not only get him fired, but thrown in jail for a long time. But I need you to tell a cop I know what happened. The video will corroborate what you say and go a long way in proving that while he did fuck a couple of other cheerleaders who did consent, you didn't."

She nods again but says nothing. After a few moments, she looks up at me and wipes her eyes. "I told my mom." She looks down. "She didn't believe me. She told me not to make waves for her in her new town."

"Then I'll figure out a way to take her down, too."

She looks up at me with wide eyes. "What?"

30

"She's part of this. Asking you to stay quiet after a teacher assaulted you?" I shake my head.

She bites her lip again and plays with the grass next to her. "I could live with my grandma and grandpa. And go back home to my old school." She pauses before taking a breath and looking up at me once more. Her green eyes are watery. "You and Dylan and all the guys are really nice, but I hate it here. I love my small town. Everyone knew me there." She shrugs. "Everyone liked me. They knew it wasn't my fault my dad died. They didn't treat me any differently. But everyone knew my mom had a hand in it. Somehow."

I chuckle. I don't know much about Rosie's story, but I do know that she moved here just before school started this year. She hasn't been here long. Only a couple of months. But rumors flew pretty quickly about why she and her mother came here from her small town somewhere near the Eastern border of Texas. Her dad died pretty suspiciously, but the police were never able to pin it on her mom. Even though they tried. Rosie thinks they're still trying. I hope they are.

I look down at my phone I put in the grass beside me and smile when I see Colton's number. My heart starts beating faster as I pick it up. Maybe he'll know or be able to find out about Rosie's case, too. Not that I want to make him feel like I'm using him, but I like the thought of him being able to help her in all the ways she needs to be helped.

Selfishly, though, I also like the thought of him being close.

Chapter Four

☪ Colton ☪

"Hey, Detective Sweet Ass. You at the school?"

I nearly choke at the nickname because it proves that Xavier was checking out my ass and that I wasn't just imagining him calling me that before. It makes me smile not just at his voice, but also at the fact that I wasn't the only one ogling that night. I may have been hiding it behind an asshole facade, but it's nice to know I wasn't wrong when I noticed him staring at me just as hard as I was him.

It's been a week since I've seen or heard from him. Fuck if I didn't miss him. I can't explain how I feel so drawn to him. I can't stop thinking about him. Which pisses me off because I should not be having feelings about a high school student. It doesn't matter that he's eighteen. He's still a lot younger than me. He lives with his parents. He doesn't even have his diploma. But none of that has stopped me from getting off to thoughts of him. That comment, though, makes me wonder if he has to me, too.

I run a hand down my face and shake my head. I can't think about shit like that right now. "I just got your message. I can be there in a few minutes. I'm not far away. What's going on?" I turn my car towards the school.

"Don't want to discuss it over the phone. We're near the entrance to the football field."

I raise an eyebrow. "Consider my curiosity peaked. I'm a couple blocks away."

"When you get here, you'll see us against the school. A little ways away from the ticket booth."

"Just stay on the phone with me. I'm not far. When you see me, you can direct me. You know what my car looks like." I can't explain the need to keep him on the phone anymore than I can the stupid urge I have to kiss him.

"Sure. A black Ford POS."

I chuckle. "Maybe if I crack my case, I'll get one of those new Dodge Chargers."

"Christ. Those are worse." Xavier laughs. "I thought departments were getting rid of those cars because of how much they suck?"

I laugh because he's absolutely correct. "I'll probably get an Impala out of the damn deal."

"Even worse!"

I laugh as I turn into the lot and head towards the football field. "Alright, I'm here."

"I see you. Keep coming this way. We're on the grass by the building. I'm waving."

I look around for him and spot him just where he says he'd be. He's smiling widely and waving erratically, but my attention falls to the girl sitting next to him. His arm is around her, but she's hugging her knees and curled into herself. I don't know what's going on, but cop instincts instantly kick in.

"I see you. Parking now."

I pull up in the fire lane, not really caring that I'd ticket people for doing what I just did. If there's a fire, I'll be a good boy and move. For now, though, the lot is full because of the game. I'm not parking three blocks away and walking when whatever he called me for has to do with that girl.

A cheerleader. She's dressed in uniform. I question why she's not on the field with the rest of her squad. But then I have the same question about Xavier. He's an All-Star Quarterback. I looked up his stats because

I'm apparently a stalker now, too, and not just a man who has unexplainable feelings for a guy he doesn't even really know.

Xavier not only leads all high school students in the State as best quarterback, he also rivals college students. Above and beyond that, there are talks he might just be the greatest high school quarterback of all time. He's good. Very good. So, why he's dressed in jeans and a red t-shirt that shows off all of his toned body is something I'm not following. I guess I'm about to find out, though.

"What's going on? How come you're not playing?" I ask as I kneel in front of them.

"Colton, this is Rosie. She's a cheerleader on the Varsity squad. She's really good. She's sixteen."

I raise an eyebrow as Xavier talks, silently questioning where he's going with that lead in, but I focus on Rosie. "Hey, Rosie. I'm Colton DeLise. I'm a detective with BSPD." I speak kindly, keeping my voice low and friendly, and reach out a hand for her to shake.

She doesn't look up at me, but she does take my hand. Hers is trembling as she shakes it lightly and lets it go. "Rosie," she whispers. She goes right back to hugging herself.

Xavier hugs her closer to him and looks at her with a comforting smile. "Colton is a friend. Can I tell him?"

She shrugs and nods slowly. "If you trust him." She sniffles.

"I do." Xavier hands me his phone. "That video is from a Go Pro camera we have set up in a classroom of a teacher."

My eyes widen. "Why would you set a camera up to spy on a teacher?"

He nods to his phone. "Just watch. I have the full video from the past week saved to a couple of flash drives."

I glance at the phone then back up at him. Then I look back down at his phone as I shift and sit down. "What am I about to watch?" I hit play on his screen.

"Something that will shock the ever living fuck out of you. I'll tell you that."

He's not wrong. "Holy… fuck…" My eyes about bulge out of my head, and I have to fight myself to keep my mouth from dropping open. Rosie shifts so she's hiding her face in Xavier's chest. I shake my head. "This is a teacher here?"

Xavier nods. "The first girl is a cheerleader. She's eighteen. You can't hear the audio too well on my phone, but she's talking shit about my cousin, Dylan, who is also a cheerleader. Right after that, she goes down on him."

"In the fucking classroom." I'd growl, but I'm shocked as hell. The video changes to another girl. "This girl is different."

"She's just eighteen. He eats her out right before she blows him."

I glance up at Rosie when she makes a choking sound. Xavier just hugs her tighter. I don't like what I know I'm about to see. "Why did you set this up?" I ask as I look back down at the video.

"Dylan refused to dissect a fetal pig. A few of the other girls refused as well. He let them slide, but not Dylan. She told her dad. He said he'd take care of it. From a grade perspective he did, but Dylan suspected the girls that he allowed to slide and said nothing to were doing favors for him on the side. Or at least one of the girls were. That girl said she had a religious excuse or some shit. But we trust our cousin. While her dad dealt with the grade, we set up a camera to see if we could catch him doing something illegal with that girl. We didn't expect this."

I shake my head as he fucks a third girl. Rather she fucks him. She rides him like a fucking bucking bronco while he's on his desk. "How old is the third girl?" He has no idea how badly I want him to say under eighteen. It makes the case I'm going to file far easier.

"She's eighteen. So is the next girl."

I nod as I watch a fourth girl. I pinch the bridge of my nose. "Fuck."

"When you get to the fifth girl, mute it," He murmurs to me softly. Rosie sobs into his chest as he sways with her. "You can unmute it after her."

"After?" I look up at him. He just nods. I know I'm not going to like what I'm about to see. I already know, but now I know for certain that whatever it is will make me want to rip the guy's balls off and feed them to him.

As if on cue, Rosie enters his classroom. I watch as she hands him a paper. I couldn't really hear anything before, but I muted this one at Xavier's request, so I really can't hear anything now. Not that I need to. I was trained to read lips a long time ago. It was an extra course I took to expand my police skills. I can't say the angle is great, but I know he's telling her that she's worthless and will never pass his class. Even with the extra credit paper she's handing in.

Of course, that's not all. He almost immediately propositions her by telling her that her grade will improve exponentially if she does a few favors for him. Favors along the lines of what she did for him Friday. My assumption is that would be last Friday, considering today is Friday and this is timestamped with yesterday's date.

She looks down, so I can't see her lips, but she shakes her head. When she tries to leave, he stops her. She tries to leave several times after shaking her head. I can tell she's crying and upset. When I can catch what she's saying, it's obvious she's telling him to leave her alone. That she never wanted to have sex with him.

The next thing I know, he's shoving her to her knees. Rosie is sobbing as he makes her suck him off. I inadvertently put a hand to my mouth, but I'm glad I've done it because it covers the snarl that escapes my throat. This guy was going down before, but he's absolutely going to face the music for his actions now.

As if that wasn't enough, ten minutes after Rosie flees his classroom, another girl enters. Like the blowjob wasn't enough for him, he has to fuck this girl. Against a wall. The same one who was riding him before.

The video ends there. I shake my head as I hand Xavier back his phone. "Jesus Christ."

"I don't have video of it, but Rosie said something happened last week. It wasn't just that."

"I don't need a video of it." I scoot a little closer to Rosie. "Rosie? That video will go far, but how do you feel about giving me the nail I need to put that son of a bitch away for life?"

She sniffles and nods as she slowly looks at me. "There's more... I told Xavier, but..."

"It's about her mom," he says quietly. "I... guess I'm really hoping you can help her. No one else has."

I hold out my hand for her. It takes her a good minute, but she finally takes mine. "Let's go talk at my office."

She shakes her head. "I... don't... really trust the police here." She glances at Xavier, and I have to wonder if she knows about his dad, or if

36

something has happened to her involving the police here. Whatever it is, I intend to find out.

"Then we'll talk in my mobile office." I tilt my head towards my squad. "It's not very spacious, but it's cool. Maybe we can talk Xavier into coming with us to a park. We'll have a conversation and go from there. What do you think?" I watch Xavier stand out of the corner of my eye, but I stay focused on Rosie.

She smiles softly. "Okay."

"Good. I just need to tell Brant I'm taking off," Xavier says. He quickly jogs towards the field.

I bite my tongue to keep myself from watching his lean muscles move with his effortless motions. My attention needs to be on the terrified girl in front of me. So, I ignore my reaction to him and help her stand. I lead her to my car and wait for Xavier to return. I'm glad he's coming because he seems to be a great comfort to her. She's going to need that.

But secretly, and very selfishly, I'm happy he's coming because it means I'll get to spend more time with him.

☾★☾

I sigh and rub my head after we drop Rosie off at Dylan's house. "You think she'll be okay there tonight?" I ask Xavier as my head falls back against the headrest in my car.

"Yeah. Dylan will take care of her. It's better than with her mom."

I chuckle. Not because what he said is funny, but because he's right. Rosie told me a lot of shit that I need to take time to digest before I can even come close to helping her. Just dealing with her sexual assault and the encounters with the other students will tie me up for weeks as I build my case. Adding on what she told me about her father's death, though, is information I don't know how to deal with right now.

Huckleberry Grove, the small town Rosie is from, is nowhere near my district. It's not even in the same county. Hell. Half the town isn't even in Texas. It's in Louisiana. Maybe not half. More like the outskirts of it. Either way, it makes for a very fucked up jurisdiction for law enforcement. If Texas doesn't want to deal with it, they just say it's Louisiana's problem. And vice versa.

Regardless, I have to do something. Cops didn't listen to Rosie when they interviewed her. If they had, her mother would be in prison where she rightfully belongs. I very clearly heard every single word that came out of her mouth. Right down to the part where she said she saw her mother with a shovel that had blood on it and watched her hide it in the barn under bales of hay that they fed to their cows.

But the cops never looked. In fact, they gave the case to Louisiana. Who never did anything with it, according to what I found regarding the case. Rosie believes they are working on it but can't prove her mother did anything. The only thing they've done is rule his death suspicious. Nothing more.

And the reason it was given to Louisiana? Because her house is near the border. She's in the area the two States fight over. Reading over the case notes I was able to access through our databases pisses me off. I can't believe how lazy some cops are. It makes all of us look bad. No wonder we have such a terrible reputation.

I scrub my hands over my face. "Why didn't you tell me what was going on earlier, Xavier?" I look over at him before shifting my car into drive and heading back towards the school so he can grab his car.

He shrugs. "Because I didn't have anything to give you until today. Everyone knows that what Dylan said she thought was happening wouldn't have gotten anywhere. And I didn't know about Rosie until this morning. I've been going back and forth about telling our school officer, but I don't really like him. I guess I just had to think of who I could trust. In the end, I didn't feel like I could trust anyone but you."

I glance at him. He's focusing his attention out the windshield, but I can tell he's exhausted. On a whim, I reach over and squeeze his thigh. It's a way to show him both support and comfort, but I don't miss the quiet sound that comes from his throat; the way his thigh doesn't tense in the slightest under my touch. In fact, it's almost like I can feel him relaxing.

"You can trust me, Xavier."

He nods with a soft smile. "I know. It wasn't a matter of not being able to trust you. It was that I didn't feel like what I had was enough. For anyone. Even if I did take it to the school cop. All of those girls are eighteen. Legal. Except Rosie."

I shake my head and squeeze his thigh again as I drive. Now that I know he'll let me touch him, some fucked up part of me doesn't want to stop. "It doesn't matter if they were nineteen. They're high school students in a school he works at. In the State of Texas, it's still a crime. He's a teacher. It's illegal for him to have a sexual relationship with any of his students unless he's either married to them or less than three years older. Well, it's three years. If he was three years and a day older than them, it would still be a crime."

He looks at me in shock. "Seriously?"

I nod. "He's fucked, Xavier. Your video gives me what I need to go after him just for them. He'd get a lot of time in prison. And I'll charge him with the four counts of statutory rape, but it's Rosie's case that will get the attention from the prosecutor."

He smiles. "Good." He looks back out the window.

After a few moments, I feel his hand on mine. My heart skips a beat at his touch. I glance at him and then our hands. I want to turn my palm so it's facing up. I want to link our fingers, but I can't bring myself to do it.

Maybe it's the logical part of me kicking in for once. The part that is reasonable and understands that I'm playing with fire. Getting involved with a kid twenty years younger than me is dangerous as fuck. But I'm pretty sure it's the terrified part of me. The part that is pretty sure if I move, I'll scare him away.

"What about high school students and cops?" he asks quietly. "Can you get in trouble if…" He trails off and doesn't look at me.

My chest tightens at the prospect of his words. I clear my throat. "Depends on my role in your life. If I were the SRO at your school? I would get in trouble. Doesn't matter your age. If I have anything to do with the school or school district you attend, then yes. I can get into a lot of trouble."

"But… you don't have anything to do with my school. Do you?"

I turn into the parking lot of the high school and park near his car. It's the only one in the lot. "No. I don't."

"So…" He looks over at me a little shyly but still full of a confidence I envy. "I could kiss you right now, and there wouldn't be legal repercussions?"

I look down at his hand. He's started moving his thumb in circles over mine. My throat has suddenly gone dry, and I feel like I'm back in high school and trying to figure out how to kiss my first boyfriend without making it seem like I'm coming on far too strong.

I let my other hand fall between my legs to hopefully hide what he's doing to me, but I don't miss that he's doing exactly the same thing. I force my eyes to slowly rise. His eyes have turned so heated that the reflection of the lights in the parking lot in them make them look like they're on fire.

For me.

Dragging myself away from the cliff edge I'm about to fall off of, I clear my throat. "Not legally." I watch him smile a little more devilishly. "But that doesn't mean you should, Xavier," I nearly whisper. "At least, not right now."

Watching his face fall slightly might damn well be my undoing. Saying those words when all I want to do is taste him is the hardest fucking thing I've ever done. When he nods and opens the door, though, I fight to pull him into me and take what I want.

What *he* wants.

He's too quick, though. While I'm struggling with myself, he steps out of my car. "See you later, Detective Sexy."

He closes the door and is quickly walking to his car. It's not until he ducks inside that I realize what he just called me. Just like that, I'm smiling because it means he heard what I said.

What I didn't mean to say.

The words give us both hope. While it seems wrong to want an eighteen-year-old high school student, he won't be in high school forever. Until then, we can be friends. If the attraction is still there in a few months when he graduates, then I'm all for exploring it.

Even though it just might kill me to wait.

Chapter Five

☪ Xavier ☪

(One Month Later)

I reach for my phone when the alarm goes off and rub my eyes. It takes me a few minutes to sit up, but I finally manage to do it. It's not because I'm tired. It's because last night's game kicked my ass. I took a lot of hits, but we played hard and won. We only have one more game before the playoffs. We're still undefeated this season, but we face our toughest team and biggest rivals next week.

I yawn and open my eyes as I lean against my headboard. "Dad!" I yell in surprise when I see him sitting on my desk chair staring at me. "Fuck. What the hell?" I rub my chest to assist my heart in resuming its normal rhythm. "What are you doing?"

"The press conference for Texas A&M is today. Imagine my surprise when I found that out and hadn't received a call to set you up attending it."

It takes me a full minute to realize what he's saying. The press conference where Texas A&M announces athletes who have signed promise letters to attend their university is today. I scrub my hands over my face because I can't believe we're still having this same conversation. It's been months. We're already almost through the first semester of the school year. In just over three weeks, it will be our winter break.

"Dad. I told you. I'm not attending A&M. I have offers from all over the -"

"The other offers don't fucking matter! Get your ass out of that bed. Get dressed. And meet me downstairs."

I just blink a few times. "Why?"

He stands. "Because I spent all fucking night waking people up all to make sure my son, who forgot completely to commit to A&M, is a part of the conference he's supposed to be a part of! You have five minutes!"

I just stare at him in shock. "What is your problem? Why is A&M so fucking important to you?"

His already bloodshot eyes seem to become impossibly more red. I'd cringe, but I'm not afraid of him at all. "Move!" he screams at me. "I'm not telling you again!"

It's my turn to see red. "No! I'm not going to A&M! I'm going to Brystone Springs! I already committed! Now, get the fuck out!"

I swear to fuck he levitates off the ground, grows horns and a tail, and launches at me without touching the ground. His entire face turns as red as my boxer briefs. I see it coming, though, and dodge the attack. I roll out of bed and hit the ground just as he lands in the bed with his hands around my pillow. My eyes widen when I realize he would have started choking me.

My dad, still quick on his feet, launches again. But this time, he gets tangled in my blankets and crashes into the wall. His hand hits my nightstand, sending books and my lava lamp flying. In his struggle with the blankets, his foot crashes into the nightstand. It topples on top of him.

But it only infuriates him more. "Son of a bitch!" he screams. "When I get my hands on you, I'm going to fucking kill you! Understand me?"

I know I don't have a lot of time to get away from him without getting into a fight. So I grab a pair of jeans and pull them on as he's fighting to stand. I find a t-shirt and grab it, my phone, keys, and wallet.

Just as I reach my door and open it, a hard body shoves me into the wall. "Fuck!" I yell. He spears my hair and shoves my head into the wall. I drop my phone and everything else in my hand as the pain radiates from my temple, through my head, and down my arm and back.

"You think you can just walk out? Huh?" He pushes me harder against the wall. "That you can just leave and go to whatever college you desire? Even though you were already promised to A&M?"

"What?" I shake my head and use all my strength to shove back. His grip loosens, but he just readjusts. One arm is suddenly around my neck. The other is around my torso.

"You think after all I've been through that I'll just let you walk away from A&M? Is that what you think?"

I struggle against his hold. "What the hell are you talking about?"

"You have no choice, you spoiled fucking prick! You have no choice because I don't!"

His words send my mind into a tailspin, but it's the fact that he's cutting off my air supply that really starts to scare me. So, I start fighting back with everything I am. I headbutt him. I elbow his ribs. I wiggle and squirm like my life depends on it because it fucking does.

When I get free, I jump up and turn as quickly as I can, but he's already on his feet. I dodge a hit and shove him backwards. He lands on the bed again. It gives me time to grab the heaviest book that I have, my history book, and swing it as hard as I can at his head just as he stands and lunges again. He immediately slumps to his knees with a groan. I'm about to swing it again, but he falls to his side.

I don't waste a second. I grab my backpack and shove all of my books and school work into it. I find my gym bag with my gear and uniform from last night. He groans a few times while I'm getting my shit together, so at least I know he's not dead. I grab a second gym bag and start throwing clothes into it. I don't know where I'm going, but I'm not staying in this house anymore.

I grab all of my bags and a pair of shoes along with my wallet, keys, and phone I'd dropped just as he's making his way to a sitting position. He gingerly touches the side of his head and looks at his finger to see the blood.

"You just killed me, you know."

I narrow my eyes. "Fuck you. You look just fine to me."

I don't say another word. I walk away as quickly as I can, glancing over my shoulder to make sure he's not following me. I jog down the stairs and through the living room towards the door to the garage. I roll my eyes when I see my mother passed out on the couch. Same place she was when I got home last night. I'd say I can't believe that she didn't wake up, but I know better.

I hurry to the garage. I don't want to give him a chance to recover enough to come after me. Hopefully, I'll be long gone by then. I throw everything into my car and take off. I don't really know who to go to, though.

After last night's win, Sterling, Drake, Kody, and Brant all went on a camping trip. The only reason I didn't go is because it meant I'd have to drive a very long way to get to Kody's family cabin. The cabin is nearly two hundred miles from here. And then, because we've never liked staying in the cabin unless we've needed to, we would have had to set up our tents on the property in the dark. I wasn't in the mood.

Dylan has Rosie at her house still. Over the past couple of months, Rosie has basically moved in. Not like her mom gives a fuck. Turns out she has a sexual relationship going on with the teacher who assaulted her daughter. Or so she says. We all question that. Even Rosie, who never saw them together. Whatever her game is, though, it disgusts me. It disgusts us all.

The teacher, though, did get charged with a multitude of crimes. Colton was right. With everything brought against him, I don't think that fucker will see the light of day. I was not happy when the prosecutor dropped the charges against him for the other four girls, but in the end, I understand. He has a strong case with them and the video evidence, but he can get more time if he goes after him for what he did to Rosie. Rosie is being incredible and so strong during all of this.

The girls involved in not only bullying Dylan and Rosie, but also fucking the teacher, all got expelled from school and kicked off the cheerleading squad. Dylan became head cheerleader. There's talks about the team going to Nationals this year. Not only would that look incredible for Dylan, but it makes her happy. Things on that front are coming up roses.

Colton, though, has gotten a lot busier. He wasn't kidding when he said his case was blowing up. There's a lot of shit going on in this city, but he was right about Onyx. The owner was dealing drugs and had an illegal weapons trade going on. Onyx was bought by some hotshot who lives in

Chicago and owns a few clubs. Passion projects apparently. The guy is a billionaire in some industry. Cooper Hayden or something.

Colton and I still make time to talk and text. We even hang out a little bit, and he's managed to make it to every game I've played. Including the away ones. We tease each other a lot and flirt even more, but we both agree that until things calm down from the fallout with the school's sex scandal, it would be best to keep our relationship friendly.

Not that that's easy in the slightest. I always have to check myself from letting myself push him too far. I'm not stupid, though. I know he does the same. We've been close to kissing several times. We always manage to stop ourselves, but it's getting a lot more difficult. I want him. I know he wants me. We keep telling each other that it's best to stay friends, but I don't know if that excuse will keep working for much longer.

I smile a little thinking of him. Just his eyes do things to me that no other has. My reaction to him freaks me out while, at the same time, makes me want to explore every inch of it. Which I'm sure is a lot of inches.

I reach down and squeeze my growing cock with a groan. Yeah. Like that's normal. Get into a fight with my dad. Get an erection five minutes later while in the process of trying to figure out where the fuck I'm going to go since I won't be going home. But it's like my dick is trying to tell me what my heart already knows. There is someone that I can reach out to. Someone I know will help me without hesitation.

Colton.

I sigh and pull over into the parking lot of the school. I take out my phone and put it on speaker. I could just use the Bluetooth and keep driving, but I don't know where I'm going. I hate not having a direction. I've been to his place before, but I don't know if he'll welcome me there or not. Maybe he's not there. I don't know.

"Hey, All-Star. What's up?"

I smile at Colton's deep voice and shiver just like I always do when I hear it. "Just fought with my dad. Almost knocked his ass out. I thought I killed him for a minute."

"Whoa. Hold up, cowboy. What the fuck?"

I sigh and rub my head as I close my eyes. "I woke up like I always do on a Saturday morning. I slept an extra hour. You know. Normal shit for me. I was getting up. Just about to get out of bed and grab my workout clothes. Then hit the gym for my workout. My dad was sitting on my desk chair staring at me. It looked like he hadn't slept or was still drunk. I couldn't decide which right away. At least not until he started yelling at me about A&M and how their press conference is today. How he never got a call about me being involved like I was supposed to be."

Colton groans, but it sounds more like a protective growl. I swallow hard and look at my phone as he clears his throat. "He found out about BSU."

"Not exactly." I lean my head back against the headrest and close my eyes as I shake my head. "I ended up telling him. He attacked me."

"He what?" He makes a dangerous sound. There's no doubting it was a growl, and it makes my eyes snap open. "Where are you? Did you leave?"

"Uh… yeah. I grabbed some of my shit and my school stuff. I took off."

"Where are you? Did you go to one of your cousins?"

I sit up a little straighter. There's something about his tone that both turns me on and makes me actually feel how much he cares. "No. They're camping. And with everything going on with Rosie and Dylan, I don't want to go there. Unless it's a last resort. I guess I could drive up to Kody's cabin, but it's quite a drive. I could probably stay at one of their houses, but I don't want my dad to show up and fuck with them. He just might. He said a lot of shit that I didn't understand while we were fighting."

"Just… come here. Come to my place. You know the code. It's the same to get into the private garage. Tell me when you're here, and I'll come down. You can't come up without a keycard. It'll save you a trip to the lobby. I need to remember to get you a key."

My heart quickens a little. "A key?"

"Well, yeah. You're here enough. Listen, I need to go. I'm home. Just in the middle of something. Call me when you get here." He hangs up.

I sit and blink at the phone a few moments before the mentality to drive the car finally comes back to me. He has my mind racing as fast as my heart. A key? To his penthouse? It's more like a mansion in the sky. I mean, we've become close, and I want things to go further, but the fact that he wants to give me a key, that he trusts me with one, makes me feel like I'm flying.

I smile as I drive to his place. It's not quite downtown, but it's close. It's really nice with a lot of security features. Like I can't access the elevator without a particular keycard. The only ones who have that key are security guards or the residents. As a guest, I have to be on an approved list for the guards or have Colton meet me in the lobby. Each keycard is different for each floor, but a code is also needed. If someone loses their keycard, random people can't try to get in without the code.

Which is one of the reasons I'm close to my heart escaping out of my chest. Colton trusting me with his code to get into the building, so I didn't have to wait to be buzzed in was one thing. But wanting to actually give me a keycard is something else entirely. My stomach tightens. My chest feels like it might burst. I can't wait to see him. I just might not be able to resist the urge to kiss him for this.

I wonder if he'd stop me or kiss me back. I've never blushed in my life, but I feel the heat creeping into my cheeks thinking of his tongue. Not that I don't think of what it would be like to kiss him each and every day. Or where that kiss would lead. But something about thinking of actually doing it as soon as I see him makes it all feel different.

More real.

Maybe if I take that step, he'll see that I'm ready. That I've been ready. That there's really no reason to hold back. He doesn't work for the school. I'm eighteen. There's nothing stopping us from giving into the attraction that we both have for each other. What's the point of just teasing each other and testing limits with touches here or there? Or heated gazes while we stare at each other's mouths? I get the reasons we were waiting, but the more I think of them now, the more I'm just sick of waiting.

When I get to Colton's, I've talked myself into kissing him. I'm sick of waiting. He makes me feel like an out of control wildfire. He's the only cure for the inferno he has me in a constant state of. I call him and wait for him to come down. He's deep in conversation on his phone, but he grins when he sees me and waves me in the elevator.

I'm anxious, but I behave. I keep my bags in my grip and lose myself in my thoughts. I don't know what he's discussing, but I know it's important because of the way he's talking. It sounds like some kind of a plan is being set into motion. Cop stuff. He'll tell me later. I love hearing about it and feel pretty good about being the one he can talk to about it all. That he trusts me with it.

Just as the doors open on his floor, he hangs up and smiles at me again. My heart melts. "Good news. I got more outside help to help me clean up the department. People who've done it all over the country. They're good."

I follow him off the elevator. "That's good news."

"Even better is that they're going to help with Rosie. I've done just about all I can, but they don't have a jurisdiction to worry about."

I raise an eyebrow. "So, the FBI? They don't have jurisdiction, do they?"

He unlocks his door. "Not the FBI. Better. One of the guys on the taskforce I put together recommended them. He works with them. They're…" He trails off and looks down at me. "They're sort of like Black Ops." He pushes the door open.

"Good. We can use all the help we can get for her."

I follow him inside his penthouse and close the door. I drop my bags and, before I lose my courage, grab his arm. When he turns, I kiss him. I crush my lips to his in a kiss that only manages to ignite the fire inside me instead of quenching it in the slightest, even though his lips aren't moving against mine.

Was I wrong?

Did I read his attraction incorrectly?

Did he not admit it?

Did we not talk about it?

Did I imagine it all?

I watch his eyes widen in shock before his hands grip my hips. I think he's about to push me away, but he doesn't. He backs me against the door and moves his mouth against mine hungrily. His tongue slips past my lips and dives in, tangling with mine. I close my eyes and groan. My arms wrap tighter around his broad shoulders. I didn't even know I'd moved them there.

He pulls me closer to him while simultaneously crushing me against the door behind me. His large hands grip my ass as he angles his head. He presses against me and moans into the kiss as he deepens it further. I can feel his reaction to me grinding against my own hard cock.

Colton pulls away slowly, leaving us both breathless. All doubt I had in my mind about his feelings for me vanishes completely. Reflected in his eyes is the same desire I have for him. The insane attraction I had for him since the second I saw him has grown so much, but right now, it's simmering right below the point of explosion.

I need him.

I need Colton DeLise.

Chapter Six

☾★ Colton ★☾

Fuck…

Oh, fuck…

I take deep breaths and watch Xavier. Holy fuck. I've never felt like my entire fucking world was exploding around me with just a kiss, but that's exactly what just happened. I've never allowed myself to lose control like that, but I did with him. And I didn't give one single fuck. All I cared about was him. His tongue. His body pressed against me. His hard as hell cock grinding against mine.

"Christ, Colton," Xavier whispers. He runs his thumb over his lip as he grins.

I take a few steps back. "Holy shit," I whisper.

"Colt!" someone yells from somewhere in my penthouse.

"Fuck. Gavin." I shake my head like I'm coming out of a haze.

"Who's Gavin," Xavier asks. I can see the sudden hurt replace the lust that was there moments ago. "A boy-"

"No. No, baby. Not a boyfriend." I scrub my hands down my face at the slip of calling him baby, though it was the most natural fucking thing I've ever done. Second only to kissing him. "Fuck," I groan. I drop my hands to my sides and glance at his bags before looking back at him. Thankfully, the hurt I saw that tore me apart is gone. "Let's… uh… Let's get your stuff to your room."

He watches me as I pick up his bags. I'm pretty sure he's still reeling from the mind-blowing kiss. I know I am. I turn and quickly make my way to my guest bedroom. I open the door and let out a breath as I stride to the bed. I put his stuff down and turn around to face him. That kiss, while absolute fire, can't happen again. At least, not now. He has more important things to worry about.

I mean to tell him that, but when his eyes meet mine and he smiles, I can't find the words. "I probably shouldn't have assumed that when you said to come here, it meant to bring all my shit with," he says. He tries to portray confidence, but I know him better than that. I can hear how unsure he is.

"I did mean that, Xavier," I say, my voice thick.

I look down because I don't want him to see the war raging in my eyes. I *want* to kiss him again. I want to do a lot more with him, but it's not the time. We both have a lot going on. I feel like starting a relationship would be a stupid decision, but I also don't care.

When I look back up, he's smiling once more. It strikes me quite suddenly that I'm not the only one of the two of us who is in territory he isn't familiar with or comfortable in. Xavier and I have talked quite a bit about things over the past couple of months. He's usually the one in control. He knows what he wants. He doesn't hold back, but he has with me.

I know how it must make him feel unsure because I feel exactly the same way. I know where I want to go with him, but things are so different with him. He's not just anyone to me. I've had a couple of relationships and fast fucks. He's not a fast fuck or anything like any other man I've been with. He's more.

He's everything.

I clear my throat. "I should probably get back out there." I look back up at him. "We were discussing a few things."

He nods and shoves his hands in his pockets. He rocks back and forth on his heels and looks at the floor. "I'll just hang out in here. Stay out of your way." He's still smiling, but I know he wants to be out there helping. He loves not only hearing about my job, but helping when I get stuck. I like that he brings fresh ideas to the table.

"You don't have to. I'm not hiding anything from you."

"You sure?" He looks at me hopefully with a half smile.

"I'm positive. Besides, I'm sure you're starving. I was just making breakfast. Should be about done."

His smile brightens. "Okay."

I lead him out to the kitchen. "Take a seat." I nod to the table and head for the oven, where I have bacon, ham, cheese, hashbrowns, and tomatoes baking. "Gavin. This is Xavier Remington. His dad is one of the ones on that list I gave you." I pull the hashbrowns out.

"List?" Xavier asks as he sits down.

"Yeah," I say. I start dishing up the hashbrowns. "We were talking about how we thought a lot of what is going on is suspicious as fuck. Add in your father and how he's the department's golden child, even though none of us like him much. It's got our instincts telling us something just ain't right in this city." I set a plate down in front of him and Gavin. "This is Gavin Vandenberg. The help I was telling you about on the way up."

"The Black Ops guy?" Xavier smiles.

Gavin laughs as I put drinks down for us and sit down. "Sure, kid. Black Ops."

Xavier's eyes narrow slightly as he looks between us. "Why do I feel like I'm missing something? And don't call me kid. I'm eighteen. Not a kid."

I pause with an eyebrow raised and my fork halfway to my mouth. Gavin mimics me as we both stare at Xavier. Gavin might be a little shocked, but I'm in awe. And of course that awe goes directly to my dick. Good thing no one can see how hard that just made me.

"Okay. Not a kid. Xavier. I apologize." Gavin nods his head in both acknowledgement and apology, moving the fork the rest of the way to his mouth. I watch as his face lights up. "Damn. This is good. Might rival my boss. Might not believe it, but Josh Lucinio can cook. Breakfast at least. We're still working on the rest."

Xavier puts his fork down on his plate. "Lucinio. As in Lucinio Mafia?"

I drop my fork as my eyes snap to his. "You... know who Lucinio Mafia is?"

He looks at me like I'm insane. "My father is a cop. Remember? Besides, I'm not just a stupid kid. I read and watch the news. I know what the Lucinio Mafia does. My laptop has Lucinio Tech antivirus on it. They're the best." He goes back to eating as Gavin and I look at each other.

After a few moments, we both go back to eating, but it's in silence. Maybe I didn't give Xavier as much credit as I should have. He seems to know quite a lot more about the world than most people his age. Maybe that's where a lot of my hesitation about us has stemmed from. I assumed he was more naive than he actually is for his age. I've been doing him a disservice by thinking that way.

Fuck, I've been doing myself a disservice.

When we all finish, Xavier gets up and takes our plates. Why that makes me more attracted to him is far outside my scope of understanding. And something I'll need to figure out later because I have a lot larger problems on my plate right now that need to be addressed.

"So, Gavin. What do you think?" I ask, attempting to get my mind off how hot Xavier looks washing dishes.

"Well, you have a classic case of police corruption. From what I've seen and had the chance to research, a lot of the cops on this list have huge gambling problems. It doesn't surprise me that they'd be involved in shit to pay off their debts."

"Wait. Debts?" Xavier grabs a towel and turns around, drying his hands. "My dad said something that confused the fuck out of me. But gambling debts. That actually makes sense."

"What did your dad say?" Gavin asks.

"Well, we got into a fight this morning. He wants me to go to Texas A&M. I don't want to. I already signed a promise letter to Brystone Springs University. They hold their press conference next week to announce their recruits. A&M is today. My dad didn't know why he didn't get a letter about it or a call to set up my part of it. He said something about me not having a choice because he doesn't. I had no idea what the fuck he meant. Then after I hit him with a book and got my stuff, he told me I just killed him. Do you think my going to A&M had something to do with gambling?"

Gavin leans back in his chair and taps his pen against his notebook as he stares at his laptop. After a few moments, his phone vibrates. He leans forward and looks down at it before a grimace crosses his face. He flips his phone upside down and sighs as he leans back, falling quiet again.

"There's something I remember about A&M. I need to look into it," Gavin finally says after a few moments. "It's possible."

Xavier nods and goes back to the dishes. Fuck me, I'm falling in love with him. I don't have a damn clue how he is taking all of this in stride, but I love all of it. He's showing his true colors. His strength. Maturity. Things I saw already but was afraid to admit to myself. Things I was using as a barrier to hold me back from our relationship. I was an idiot to do so because Xavier is all I've ever fucking wanted.

I rub my head as I lean back in the chair. "We know we have a problem with some of the cops. Probably his dad. You think you can help?"

"I know we can. But it's not just the cops in this city. From what I've managed to figure out so far, a lot of the higher ups in this city are on the take, too. With who? I don't know that yet. But given what I do know?" Gavin looks at me seriously. "I need to call in the boss. Because I have a very bad feeling that this is just going to get worse. This entire city is seriously corrupt."

I nod. "I was afraid you'd say that."

Xavier comes back to the table drying his hands. "What about Rosie?" He sits down and looks at Gavin just as seriously as Gavin had me moments ago.

Gavin nods. "Rosie is a whole other aspect to this. A different issue altogether. I already have some people working on that." He looks back at me. "I also want to bring in some men for protection. Going after that teacher has brought attention to you that you didn't need with your current investigation." Gavin's eyes flick to Xavier and back to me. "And considering your connection to Xavier? There's a high chance that he'll have people going after him, too. If not from those with their eyes on you, then from whatever the fuck his dad is neck deep in."

Xavier glances at me and chuckles. "I guess I was right to call you."

"I hope you would have anyway," I say quietly with a soft smile.

Gavin chuckles, bringing us both back from whatever world we sunk into where only each other exists. "I need to make some calls."

"You can use the living room if you want somewhere quiet," I say. I nod to Xavier. "You should probably call Dylan and Rosie."

Xavier watches Gavin stand and head for the semi-closed off living room. "I should call my cousins. All of them. We're all close. They won't want to be kept out of this. If there's going to be some big plan coming together, I'll want them around. Especially with the mafia being involved and potential danger to us."

I nod. "Anything you need." I look up when I hear my buzzer signaling someone is here and head for the intercom.

"That will be Damon and Lance," Gavin says with a chuckle from my couch. "Call them Cute and Quirky when you answer the intercom."

I raise an eyebrow. "That was fucking fast. Didn't you just call them in?"

He raises his phone slightly. "Boss looked into this a little. He thought we'd need backup. He's finishing a few things in Chicago. Then, he's coming down here. Cleaning up an entire city is going to take time and a fuck lot of work. We might end up calling in the Crane's on this one. Might be an idea to get them down here, too. We'll need all the help we can get."

I nod as I answer the intercom. "Yeah?"

"Mr. DeLise?" one of the two asks.

I glance back towards Gavin. He nods with a smirk. I clear my throat. "Yeah. Cute and Quirky?"

I hear a voice mutter that they're gonna kick Gavin's ass before I hear a response. "That's us."

I laugh. "I'll have security let you up."

"You do that. And tell Vandenberg he's a fucking asshole, and he'd better run."

I laugh as I buzz them in. I quickly call down to security that they're okay to come up, then disappear down the hall where I saw Xavier walk to. I make my way to the guest bedroom. The door is cracked, but I pause just before opening it.

"Yeah," Xavier says. "I don't know, man. I don't know what he'll do. File an assault charge? Sounds like something he'd do. I'll probably be in jail by Monday morning. I need you guys. I'm sorry for pulling you in, but it sounds like this is going to get worse before it gets better. Especially with the mafia involved." He pauses. I peek into the room. He tilts his head as he listens. "No, I don't think you need to pull him into this. Not unless you want him here. Then again, we might need all the help we can get. I don't know. I'll leave that to you." He pauses again.

I push the door open slightly, and lean on the frame. His back is to me. I want him to turn around. Maybe I should make a noise so he doesn't think I'm eavesdropping or something.

He sighs and rubs his head. "I called Dylan. They're on their way. I just need to ask Colton if they can stay. He only has two rooms, and he put me in one of them. The other is his, and I don't think he wants to share it with me."

The fact that he thinks that breaks my heart, but I can't blame him for the thought. I didn't offer it. I haven't told him how I feel about him. It's a situation I need to rectify. Immediately. I can't let him go on thinking I don't want him. I do.

I notice a crumpled piece of paper on the table by the door. I have a random cactus I'm attached to sitting on it. I pick it up and lightly toss it. It hits the back of his head dead center. He jumps and turns to me. I just smile.

"Hey, I gotta go. Colton just threw something at me to get my attention. When you're back, give me a call." He pauses another moment before he says goodbye and hangs up.

I crook my finger at him but stay right where I am. I hear Gavin answer the door and Damon and Lance enter my penthouse, but they aren't what matters to me right now. The sexy guy strutting towards me is all that's important.

When he reaches me, I cup his face in my hands. I lean in and kiss him. Slow. Deeply. I pour everything I feel for him into it, so he can't think for one second that I don't want him. I want everything with him. I need him more than the air I breathe. Christ. He is my air. Without him, I don't think I could even manage to get my lungs to inflate; my heart to beat.

And while all of that scares the fuck out of me, at least the part about feeling it for someone half my damn age, there's one thing I'm certain of. Xavier is my person. The only one I want. All I need. I swipe my tongue over his and wrap my arms around him, deepening the kiss even more, because I need to show him that I want him. Only him. No one else in this world can ever fulfill my heart and soul as he does.

I pour all of me into the kiss because it's what we both need. When I pull away, my head feels like it might explode. My heart is beating too hard. My entire body has erupted with tingles. My dick is jutting against my zipper. I'm hard as granite.

I take one of the hands Xavier has fisted my shirt in and slowly move it down my body to the waistband of my jeans. "This…" I start moving it lower and grin a little darkly when his eyes widen. "Is what you do to me, baby." I stop moving his hand when we reach my dick.

His gaze drops. "Fuck…," he whispers.

I squeeze his hand over my length just so he has no doubt in his mind what I'm telling him. "I want you, Xavier. Fucking *want* you. More than I've ever wanted anyone in my life." I squeeze his hand over my dick again. I groan low. "Look at me."

His head snaps up. His molten silver eyes meet mine. "Colton…"

"I don't want any doubt in your mind how I feel about you. I put you in this room, baby, because I wasn't sure if we were ready to take that step. I wasn't sure if I was. But I am. I knew the second I saw you that you were it. Scared me to death. The age difference. You being in school. Situations surrounding not only our meeting but our whole goddamn relationship." I release his hand and slowly caress mine up his arm to his bicep until I reach his neck. "I don't care anymore. All I care about is you."

Xavier wraps his arms around my neck and pulls me in to kiss me again. It's slow. Far more heated. I suck on his tongue and nip his lip just before I pull away, but I'm not quite ready to release him. So, I pull him closer and hug him for I don't know how long before I finally let him go. I reach down and grab his bags, still sitting on the floor just inside the room. I bring them to my bedroom and set them inside the door before turning to him again.

His eyes.

I could fucking drown in them and die happy. It's a thought I've had so many times, I've lost count. They're bright. Mischievous. Purely Xavier.

And all mine.

Chapter Seven

☪ Xavier ☪

Fuck... Fuck... Fuck... Fuck... Fuck...

He's... Oh, fuck.

I swallow hard as I watch Colton. He doesn't move, but the way he's looking at me makes me want to spontaneously combust. I can't breathe. I can't think. Well, that's not true. I can think. I can think of his hard cock under my palm. My heart stopped beating in that very moment. I can think of his heated gaze on me right now. And the nice tent my jeans are making in this very moment. Similar to the one his are making, but not as big.

Christ.

I've always thought I was big. Thick. But compared to him? Jesus. He has to be twice my girth. I know he has some length on my almost nine inches. All I want is his cock in my hand again. My mouth. My ass. Anywhere I can get him, I'll gladly take him. I'll even beg for it. And I don't beg. Fucking ever.

Colton stalks towards me as he glances down the hall towards the voices of Gavin and his crew. He must decide they aren't going to bother us because when he reaches me, he takes my hand and tugs me into his bedroom.

Our bedroom?

I'm already fucking thinking about where I'll keep all my stuff. Where I'll park my car. What I'll make him for dinner every night, even though he's a far better cook. I'd do it just to show him how much I care about him.

Love him?

Hell. Maybe.

Probably.

Who am I kidding?

I love him. I really fucking love him.

My throat is so dry that I can't speak. All I can do is watch him and wait for whatever he does next. I'm afraid to even move for fear I'll wake up from whatever dream I just fell into. I don't want it to end. I want to see how far he's going to take this.

He closes the door behind us and walks to his King size bed. The bedspread is dark blue. The accents are wooden and match the dark furniture in the room. My mouth can't decide if it wants to water or feel like I'm swishing sand around in it. He sits down and crooks a finger at me.

I lick my lips. Much like in the guest room, which feels like years ago, my body moves towards him on its own. My heart speeds up. My cock jerks, like it's leading me towards him. A beacon in the turbulent waters that is my life.

I don't know how or why things got so fucked up, but I do know that if they hadn't, I wouldn't have met him. I wouldn't know these feelings I have because no one has come close to giving me them. Only him. I don't want to feel like this about anyone else. I never will.

I stop in front of him, unsure if I should step between his legs like I want to, but he doesn't leave me guessing for long. He grips my ass and pulls me closer. I expect him to drop his hand when he looks up at me, but he doesn't. He leaves it right where it is and grips my ass tighter.

"You drive me crazy," he rasps. "Fucking insane. I can't even think about you without getting hard. I can't sleep without rubbing one out to thoughts of you. Every. Fucking. Night."

My mouth drops a little because I thought I was the only one. Teenage hormones and all that shit. "Really?" I ask, though it sounds a little like a squeak in a tone that's foreign to my ears. I need to get a fucking grip, but the only grip I want is on his dick while he's fucking my mouth.

He starts lightly caressing my ass. "What about you, Xavier? How many times have you thought about riding me while I'm stroking your cock until you come?"

I can feel my eyes widen. My heart accelerates even faster. "How do you... I've never... Fuck, Colt. I've always been top."

His realization knocks the cocky smirk right off his face. "Shit... Xav-"

I don't let him finish. I can't hold back anymore. I need his lips on mine. Anywhere on me will do. I knock him back on the bed and straddle him as I kiss him. Where his kiss was assertive, mine is aggressive. I want him. All of him. I don't even care.

His arms lock around me. He pulls me flat against him, but it's a huge mistake because now we can both feel each other's hard cock. I kiss him harder and grind against him, getting harder. He matches my tongue stroke for stroke. He counters me moan for moan. When I grind down, he thrusts up against me. When I nip, he nips back.

When he's had enough of relinquishing the control he desperately needs, he lets out a low growl and flips me on my back so quickly and effortlessly, it leaves me dazed. For a second, all I can do is blink at him. But then I feel his hand on my jeans. He's ripping open the button as he kisses me. With one hand, he holds my throbbing dick in place. With the other, he yanks my zipper down.

I sit up just enough to tug my shirt over my head and throw it off. My eyes roll back when he tugs my jeans down just enough to free my dick. I sit back up and reach for his jeans, fully planning on pulling them down so I can see what he's packing.

Colton pushes me back down on the bed, though. "Don't you dare."

My dick twitches at his tone, and I narrow my eyes. "Colt, if you don't do something about my hard cock, I'm shoving it in your mouth."

He just gives me a wicked grin as he tugs off his shirt. "Hasn't your mama ever told you that good things come if you wait?"

I laugh as I watch him. Colton is all hard ridges and perfect muscles. "Fuck. My mama barely taught me how to tie my shoelaces. I learned my manners from my imaginary dinosaur friend."

He laughs as he tugs down his jeans. I love his laugh, but holy shit, I love his dick even more. My eyes zero in on it as he fists it in his hand. "Is that why you're so brash? Learned your manners from a growly fucking dinosaur?"

I grin but don't get to say anything because his mouth is on mine once more. His kiss is punishing this time, but it's his dick against mine, finally, that sends my head spinning into delicious pleasure. Delirium that only he can give me.

"Oh, fuck….," I moan into his mouth as we grind against each other. I grip his ass, begging for him to get closer. "Fuck, Colt. I'm not going to be able to hold on much longer." The familiar tingle makes its way down my spine. My dick gets harder. Thicker.

"Not yet, baby," he rumbles against my neck. He reaches between us and grips both of our dicks in his large hand. "I'll make it worth the wait."

I jerk into him. "Colt, good fuck. Oh, shit, I'm gonna come."

"Don't you fucking dare," he pants against my neck as he strokes us both. "Fuck, not yet, baby. Not yet."

I grip his broad shoulders and thrust into his hand. His dick against mine is better than anything I've ever felt with anyone I've ever been with. It's better than my hand and any toy I've experimented with. If his hand gripping us both and his cock sliding against mine feels this good, I wonder what it will feel like when he takes me into his mouth… And deep in his ass.

Our thrusts against each other become more erratic. His kisses along my neck and jaw; more heated. I need my hands all over him all at once, but I'm not sure where to even begin. Everything about him is hard and rough, yet somehow irresistible.

"Now. Come, baby," Colton growls. "Right now." He doesn't stop jerking both of our dicks at the perfect pace and pressure.

I pull him even closer. "Shit…, Colton!" I growl into his shoulder as I bite it. I moan and groan. My hips slam up and down as I lose my release all over my stomach and him.

Colton's head falls back. He roars, though quietly. "Oh God, Xavier!" He keeps stroking us both as we thrust into each other, but my name on his lips make me come harder. I feel like my entire body is buzzing. Like a million bees have replaced my bloodstream or something and are flying around.

When we both finally stop making a mess of each other, Colton collapses on his back next to me and rests his hand possessively on my thigh that's covered in his come. We both pant as we come down.

"Fuck, Colton," I finally have the strength to rasp out.

He chuckles. "I needed that." He squeezes my thigh and turns his head towards me with a grin. "Rephrase. I needed you."

I faintly hear the intercom go off over my euphoria. "Sounds like Dylan and Rosie just got here."

"Gavin'll take care of it. You and I need to clean up."

I watch his every move as he gets up and pulls me with him. No one has ever owned me like that, and then taken such good care of me afterwards. As he gently cleans me up before he takes care of himself, I'm struck by just how far I've fallen.

I'm never fucking letting him go.

☪ ☪ ☪

Sunday, a day I usually lounge around for the morning, is filled with a fuck ton of action I'm not at all prepared to handle before seven in the damn morning. Especially when my night was filled with Colton's mouth around my cock and mine around his.

I smile a little as I sip my coffee. The only good thing about Gavin's boss is that he was nice enough to stop at a local coffee shop and get a variety of it. I think if he arrived any earlier without it, I would have killed him. Maybe not actually killed him. But probably punched him.

Maybe.

I growl a little from where I'm perched on the arm of a chair and glare at everyone in the room as they talk. Their boss is helping Colton cook breakfast. It's another point in his favor, but I'm still pissed off at the early wake up call and ruined morning. I could be playing out more dirty fantasies with Colton.

Instead, though, I'm out here in the living room with my cousins, Rosie, and a few of Josh Lucinio's people. Everyone is having a different conversation, and I want to scream at them all to shut the fuck up until I have enough coffee in my system to think clearly.

Which I do not.

Not even close.

"You okay?" Kody asks. "You look like you might actually fuck someone up if they look at you wrong."

I smile a little as I take a drink. "I just might. We didn't go to bed until four in the fucking morning. After you all went to sleep after the movie, we couldn't. So we fucked around. Our own fault. I know. But I'm tired as hell and not in the mood for the amount of people in this penthouse. Even if it is a huge penthouse. Which I don't understand. Cops don't make that much fucking money."

Kody chuckles as he sits in the chair next to me. He rests his elbows on his knees as I look down at him. "Dylan asked him the same thing. I thought I heard something about stocks doing well for him. He invested a lot when he was younger. Smart with his money."

"That doesn't help. Now, I'm pissed off that I never thought to ask him that. Or talk to him about it. Even though I'm curious."

Kody laughs and pats my thigh. "Calm down. Don't be too much of an asshole. I know how you get. And we already have one cranky asshole right now. We don't need two."

Before I can give him some snappy as fuck retort, the intercom goes off. "I might rip the fucking thing off the wall," I growl under my breath. Knowing that Colton is busy, though, I get up to answer. "Yeah."

"Hey. Alec Cassidy for Colton DeLise."

I look for a few moments at the badass biker looking dude. I might tell him to fuck off, but I recognize the guy next to him. I grin and contemplate giving him shit. I know security put them both on the list. I could just let them in. Security will let them up.

But that's not how I roll. "Sorry. Don't recognize you," I say instead.

"If you don't open this door, shitface, the first thing I'm gonna do after greeting my boy, is shave your prized locks." Blade Cruz, the President of the Brystone Springs Viper's Venom Chapter, growls through the intercom. "And you know I fucking will, dickface."

I laugh. "You don't know how much I needed you and your asshole attitude."

"I can guess, doucheball. Now open up." He smirks into the camera. Alec is grinning next to him. I don't recognize all the guys behind them, but I know of them. They're all wearing VV patches. "I miss my boy."

"Yeah, yeah, fucker. Security will let you up." I push the button to open the door and watch as Blade pushes by Alec to get in first. I laugh when I see his hand shoot out and whack Blade on the back of the head for the shove. I turn and almost run into Drake.

"Was that Blade?" he asks hopefully. I don't often see Drake look vulnerable, but he does right now.

I chuckle and push him back in the direction of the living room. "You'll see him in a few moments. But not in the hall. Knowing you fuckers, you'll detour to a bedroom. I know you haven't gone all the way, since he was gone for your birthday, but I know you. You've been apart for at least a month."

"Three months, actually. He's been helping the lead guy in Chicago on something big." Drake grins and winks.

I laugh and shake my head. "If I don't get any action until this is done, you don't either."

Drake gives me a wicked grin. "We'll see about that."

Blade and Drake met about a year ago after Drake was in a car accident. The guy who hit Drake was drunk and fled the scene. Blade was behind him heading to VV's Ranch just outside of town when it happened. Lucky for Drake, and all of us, that Blade was around because Drake wouldn't be with us today. Blade saved his life. He pulled him from his burning car just before it exploded. It was because of Blade that the driver was caught. Blade got his plate number, and has been with Drake ever since.

I wait by the door for them to come up and watch as Colton and Josh put breakfast out on the breakfast bar in a buffet style. Everyone else is still talking and laughing. My mood, while improving, still isn't quite there. If I'm being honest, it's not because of the time of morning or even that it was a late night. It's not that I want to be all over Colton right now.

It's because I sense the danger. I know there's far more going on here than I realize. The fact that Gavin called in the big guns and their allies tells me all I need to know. While I understand why when it comes to Rosie and the BSPD, she knows about my relationship with my dad and doesn't trust those he works with, I don't know how I fit into it. I understand my dad is into gambling with some bad people, but I have no idea what it has to do with me and his need to get me into A&M.

It's been his dream since I was a kid. Not mine. But it hasn't been until I started high school that he really started pushing me. A&M. No other option. When I told him about all of the colleges that wanted me, including Notre Dame and Louisiana State, he told me it didn't matter. A&M is where I belonged. His alma mater and that's it. Given the shit he said, I don't fucking understand what it has to do with anything.

When I hear a tap on the door, I look through the peephole. I grin as I open it. "Hey, asshole," I say to Blade.

He laughs as he puts a large hand over my face and pushes me back. He strides past me and down the hall. "Not the face I'm looking for. Drake! Where are you, baby?"

I close the door feeling somehow lighter as Drake takes a running leap into Blade's arms just as he reaches the entrance to the living room. Blade is a big guy. Probably close to six feet five or six feet six. Seeing a guy who is about my height caught in a bear hug and kissed senseless would look comical, and probably does, to a lot of people. But to me? Fucking adorable as hell. Those two were made for each other.

I want that. All of it. The deep kiss when we haven't seen each other for a while. Though, I hope that's not months like those two. I'd hate that.

As the two kiss like there's no one else in the room, my eyes meet Colton's. He gives me a soft smile that makes me melt a little but also feel like the most cherished person in the room. I smile brighter, and just like that my bad mood dissipates.

I stand straighter as a realization hits me.

I have what Blade and Drake have. It's new, but it's still perfect. Our perfect.

Chapter Eight

☪ Colton ☪

I've never liked sitting in a room of people being told what to do, where I need to sit, what my role in a raid is going to be. It's part of the reason I worked so fucking hard to get to where I am and be the one leading the raids I go on. While I still have someone to answer to, I'm pretty much my own boss. I don't like authority. Never have. Probably never will.

Ironically, this meeting doesn't feel like that. When I took my colleague's advice and called in Lucinio Mafia, I knew I'd be taking a backseat to them and their operation. Everyone knows Josh Lucinio does things his way. And if people don't follow, they're kicked out of the operation, or he walks. His reputation of taking no shit from anyone is well-known. He works from the shadows.

Much like the rest of the people in this room probably do. I know of Viper's Venom, but they keep to themselves. I've never had a problem with them. Even when their rivals have tried to pin shit on them. I know Blade very well because of it. Not really anyone else in his crew, but I trust him, so I trust them. I know how he operates.

I didn't know that he was seeing anyone, though. Let alone the high school student, who is curled up in his lap, he likes to call his boy. It sort of makes me wonder if they're into that daddy/boy thing that makes me cringe and chuckle at the same time.

Kody is plastered to Dylan and Rosie. If I didn't know they were related, I'd think he has a thing for Dylan. Hell, maybe Rosie, too. Honestly, though. I think he's just that protective. I learned from Xavier that, while they are all close in age, Kody's the youngest. A little over a year younger. Just turned seventeen.

Sterling and Brant are both sitting on the floor against the wall near the girls. Alec and a couple of the guys he brought with him are leaning against a wall near the back of the room. Damon is sitting next to Lance, who I found out is Lucinio Mafia's tech guy. Apparently, he's better than the best hackers in the world, except maybe the one with Crane Mafia. I've heard rumors that he once hacked the State Department. Good thing he's on the side of right.

Seth, one of the few people in my life I trust, brings over a kitchen chair, settling it in the space between the couch and oversized chair in my living room, and turns it around so it's backwards. He sits and rests his arms over the back of it as he puts a glass of water on the table near the couch I'm on with Xavier. He's not the one who told me about Josh, but I trust this guy with my life. He's a patrol Sergeant now, but we still work closely. He's one of my best friends. I really only have a couple. They might be the only friends I got. I take the glass and down the water.

Erik, my other best friend, sits down in the oversized chair next to Seth after coming back from the bathroom and quickly takes the glass from me. He puts it on the floor between his feet. He's always been the caretaker of our group. Which some might find surprising, considering he's six feet four and built like a tank. We've been best friends since we were little. I furrow my brows at the look he shoots Seth when he turns his attention from us, but shake it off. He catches Blade's eye before turning back to me and watching me closely.

I'd say something, but I'm too fucking tired and insatiably thirsty. Considering how much I've had to drink in the past couple of hours, since Seth and Erik got here to help me out with setting things up for when everyone else showed up, I shouldn't be tired or thirsty. I've downed a couple of cups of coffee. Water. Don't know why the fuck I can't seem to get enough fluid. I guess that's something to think about after this is over.

"Drake, stop snuggling your daddy," Brant says with a smirk and chuckle.

"Shut the fuck up, you little dick squeak," Drake returns with a laugh. "I haven't seen him in months."

"Daddy's not letting him go," Blade says with a teasing grin and a wink at Drake.

Drake cracks up. "I'm not calling you daddy."

Blade hugs him closer and tighter as everyone in the room laughs. "Fuck no. I'm not into that shit." He glances at me. I guess that answered that question.

I grin. "Me neither."

"Thank fuck for that," Xavier says with a chuckle.

"I do love when you call me sir, though," Blade rumbles. I didn't think it was possible, but Drake blushes and hides in his neck.

"Not another dominant," Damon says with a chuckle to Lance. "We have too many of those in this family." He winks at Josh. Josh grins.

When Josh begins talking, everyone falls quiet and listens. He doesn't even need to stand to command the room. "Lance. You filled me in on what you found, but let's start with you telling everyone else. I don't understand that technical shit."

Xavier chuckles as he cuddles into me. I'm laying on the couch with a massive headache brought on solely from the amount of noise way too early in this house after only getting maybe an hour of sleep. I'd probably be okay if I went to sleep when Xavier did, but I couldn't do it. After finally giving into my feelings for him and not holding back, that's one less thing on my mind. But there are still twenty other problems that need to be dealt with.

So, while Josh leads this massive undertaking, I hold Xavier against my chest and bury my face in his neck as I listen. He doesn't know it, but he's a very calming force and is combating the band of monkeys marching behind my eyes.

"Well, I found a lot of shit. I'll begin with the list of cops and city officials Gavin gave me. They all have extensive gambling debts. All of them. One of them was more than willing to talk when Damon…" He glances at Damon, a dark, muscular, imposing figure who is probably not afraid to spend time in a gym, and grins. "Let's just say when Damon persuaded him a little. He told us that his debt stems from an underground betting ring. You name it, it's going down. Things from pig racing to how long it takes rattlesnake venom to kill the average man."

I raise an eyebrow. "Wait. How the fuck do they figure that out?"

"I'll give you one guess," Damon responds.

I groan and close my eyes. "Jesus fuck."

"Yep," Lance says, confirming everything going on in my head. "They find a couple of homeless men who no one will miss. Lure them with a hot meal and place to stay. After they get them relatively healthy, they send them to their deaths. Only, they don't know it. They're blindfolded and have noise canceling headphones on. They release the snakes and let them bite. Then they watch them until they die."

"I'm going to be fucking sick," Xavier says.

"Not even the worst part," Lance continues. "The worst part is that they aren't only limiting it to money as collateral. They take anything. From your dog to the fucking house. There are even rumors about virginities running around."

Xavier sits up and furrows his eyebrows as they land on Rosie. "Tell me what I'm thinking is wrong."

"Okay," Lance says. "It's wrong. Rosie, as far as I can tell, isn't involved in that aspect of things. At least, not exactly."

My eyes darken as Dylan hugs Rosie tighter. "What do you mean not exactly?" I pull Xavier down next to me again. He's not only calming the headache, he's keeping the demons threatening to surface and tear this city apart from surfacing. Thankfully, Xavier gets the hint and stays put, letting me hug him.

"I'll get to that," Lance responds. "It's a completely separate issue, and one that Alec and Blade will need to deal with. Firstly, this gambling ring. It's not limited to Brystone Springs. The lesser shit is, but this goes beyond that. The deeper people get in debt, the more desperate they become, which the people behind this know very well. College football is a huge thing in Texas."

Xavier tenses. "Mmhmm…," he rumbles on high alert.

Lance pauses before continuing. "The wins and losses are controlled completely by this group of people. And to keep suspicion of wrongdoing to a minimum, they spread out the championships the state wins."

"Texas doesn't win college championships every year," Drake says.

"No, they don't," Damon says. "That's part of the game."

Lance taps a few keys. "It's not just championships. It's game wins and losses. If they want Texas in a big game, they pay a lot of people off. If they want them to lose, they pay off the players. But it's all about what their gamblers are betting. If they have big bets on a Texas team to win…" Lance trails off and looks up at all of us.

I watch Kody sit back on the couch. "They'll pay them off to lose so they don't need to pay out. People end up in huge amounts of debt."

"Correct," Lance says with a smile. "Opposite is also true. If no one thinks the university will win the game and bet on them to lose, they'll pay off the other team to lose so the university will take the win. Again, more people going into debt." He looks up at Xavier. I inadvertently hold him tighter and more protectively. "Your dad figured it out. Texas A&M is one of the two universities in the State who are the biggest players in the scheme. The players take huge amounts of gifts and shit. The coaches take giant payoffs. It all happens at the beginning of the year so they can be controlled the rest of the season."

"Shit…," Xavier whispers. "It all makes sense now."

"Now, I haven't figured out exactly why your dad was pushing A&M. Either he figured you would tell him when you were approached to lose, given you'd be the starting quarterback." Lance shrugs. "Or he figured he could work his way up in this gambling ring by using you as leverage. Say you're his son. You'll do what you're told. Save them money in all of those perks so they'll get more of a profit. Maybe there was another reason. I don't know, but I will. I need to speak with your father. We have some guys bringing him out to Viper's Ranch as we speak. As soon as Blade gets the text, Gavin and Damon will be heading out there to get my answers."

Xavier chuckles. "Maybe I won't get a warrant out for my arrest after all."

"About that," Josh says. "You won't. My contacts down here are taking care of it. Besides that, it was self-defense from what I heard."

I close my eyes and smile against Xavier's neck when I feel him relax. He won't admit it, but the thought of being arrested for assault on his dad was terrifying to him. Even though I told him I'd never let anything happen to him, it didn't go very far in easing his fears. Knowing he'll be okay is a giant relief to both of us. I'll have to remember to thank Josh for that.

"Now, as for the meat and potatoes," Josh continues as he stands. "Colton, you mentioned that Rosie's case is going back and forth between Louisiana and Texas. Also, that there are a lot of reports seemingly missing. You're right. Lance found them this morning deep within Texas' system."

"One thing about deleting files," Lance says with a smirk. "They aren't really gone if you know where to look."

Josh chuckles. "There is overwhelming evidence that your father was killed, Rosie." He looks at her as he talks. "But it doesn't look like it was your mother who did it. At least not the actual act. She was there, though." He looks at Blade. "When Ace pulled you into the shit in Chicago, a couple of your guys went rogue."

He raises an eyebrow. "Who?"

Josh shrugs. "Not a hundred percent, but it looks like he wanted power because he went after a few people and got himself involved in the Mexican cartel. Which runs straight through Huckleberry Grove. I sent a couple of guys out there when we kept seeing mentions of Viper's Venom. Apparently, they've been terrorizing the town."

Blade narrows his eyes and growls low. "We don't terrorize towns. We might not be the nicest guys in the world, but we don't fucking hurt people who don't deserve it, or mess shit up if it doesn't need to be done."

"I know," Josh responds and nods to Alec. "VV's President is my best friend. I know how you work. We need to figure out who went rogue on you because according to the reports, Rosie's mom was seen with someone claiming to be the Chapter President."

"Description?" Blade asks.

Josh shakes his head. "Lance hasn't gotten that far. Lots of shit in the reports he did find have been redacted, completely blacked out, or deleted all together. And while those will be able to be retrieved, it'll take time. I might have to pull Robby in to help. I know Lance has taught

Damon almost everything he knows, but there's still a lot of information to go through."

Blade looks down at his phone when it goes off. "Time to go. I got the text."

Josh nods at Damon. "Go. Take Gavin."

Alec, or Ace, as I guess he's called, looks at the two bikers against the wall. "Ink. Hawk. Go with them. Whatever our Chapter needs, make sure they get it." He watches them head for the door. "Ink," he calls.

The one I assume is Ink looks back at him. "Yeah?"

"You get that overwhelming feeling, you talk to Hawk. This is your first big assignment since you've been back. Don't hold back if you need him to take over." He watches him with a concerned glint in his eye.

Ink takes a deep breath. "Got it, prez."

I raise an eyebrow but say nothing. I'm not sure what that was about, but I really don't need to. Not so long as whatever it is doesn't affect this operation and keeping Xavier and Rosie safe. Fuck, the whole town by the sounds of it.

Josh crosses his arms over his chest and looks at me. "We'll get the city cleaned up well enough, but you stay out of it. You go about your business. You investigate your cases. The busts we do belong to you. We'll keep you and your taskforce apprised of what we're doing and where. All I want from you is to show up when I tell you to, and keep the cops off my back until we're done. I don't need people I'm not working with showing up while we're in the middle of a raid or clean up. When it's all over, my team will feed you the report you'll hand in. I don't take credit for any of this. You do. By the end of this, you'll be a hero cop whether you want the title or not."

I'm quiet for a few moments before I nudge Xavier so I can sit up. I rest my elbows on my knees and let out a breath. "I'm not going to lie. I want in on the clean up. But I know how you work." I look up at him. I can feel my eyes darken. "Just clean up my city, Lucinio. I love this place. I'm not about to let it get destroyed by some unknown force of fucking evil. I want them out of my city, and away from the man I gave my heart to. I don't want them touching my family or my people with their dark as fuck ideology."

"I get it. I'll take care of them. Just be where I need you to be. Do what I tell you to do. I know my reputation is of some heartless motherfucker who takes control of everything. I might be all of that. But while I'm cleaning up, I still need to protect you, your family, and the good people who exist in this city. When I go in, I cross lines. I do the shit you can't. And how I do it is my business. I don't want you anywhere near it because when shit goes down, and it will, repercussions of my actions could come back to you. Which makes my job a lot fucking harder because then my attention is split between my job and saving your ass. Got it?"

"Got it. I'm not often the type of guy who allows someone else to lead. I hate authority. But I know how you work. I was prepared for it. I don't give a shit about being a hero cop. I just want my city back. I want it to be a safeplace. Something we can all be proud of again."

"I'll take care of it. I have a couple of my people investigating in Huckleberry Grove. Ace and Blade will be helping with that. I have other guys who will be sticking around here. More flying in." Josh gives me a nod. "We'll take care of it. I'm also leaving a couple of people here for Rosie." He turns to her. "I heard you're not staying at home."

She shakes her head. "No, sir," she whispers.

"She's staying with Dylan," Xavier says.

"My house is Fort Knox," Dylan chuckles with a shrug. "She feels safe there."

Josh nods. "Then you'll stay there. I'll put twenty-four hour security on you. Don't worry. They'll stay discreet. No one will know they're around except you. But until we figure out who the fuck this guy is that it looks like your mother is involved with, it's best to keep you away from her."

"She's sixteen. Can't exactly keep her away if her mom files a missing person's report." I rub my head. The headache is getting exponentially worse.

"Let me take care of that," Josh says to me before turning back to her. "Just trust me. I'll always make sure you know the guys on your security detail. If they tell you that you need to disappear, listen to them. If you don't recognize them, you'll have a panic button. I'll have Lance get you equipped before you leave today."

"I hate to be a dick," I interrupt. "But are you done with me? At the risk of sounding like a whiny toddler, I have a headache that could rival the Texas sky, and I might pass out."

73

Xavier rubs my thigh and launches into this caring mode I never thought I'd find so sexy. "I'll get you to bed. Josh can fill you in if you need to know anything else."

I'd smile if I didn't think my head might actually explode. I barely register Xavier helping me to my feet and asking me if I'm okay before everything goes dark.

Chapter Nine

☾ Xavier ☾

"What the fuck?" I scramble to support the sudden dead weight of my boyfriend as he passes out. Just before we hit the ground, I manage to catch us both, but I'm horrified.

Brant is at my side in a flash. "What the hell happened?" He puts Colton's arm over his shoulders and helps me support him.

All I can do is look at him, terrified, because I don't know what's going on. All I know is my heart is beating at a rate that can't be healthy. Colton didn't drink anything last night. He's not drunk. Yeah, we're both a little sleep deprived, but I've never seen anyone pass out because of it.

"He said he had a headache," I wheeze over my sudden hyperventilation. "Can headaches make people pass out like that?" A sudden thought hits me. "Oh, fuck!" I look at Brant. "Remember that kid in the news a couple years ago? He got tackled. Next thing anyone knows, he's dead. Brain aneurysm." The idea doesn't help me calm down. I jump when I feel a hand on my back.

"Get him to the bedroom," Josh says calmly. "Lay him down. I'll call a doctor." He looks over at Lance. "Help them. Make sure he's still breathing."

"On it." Lance shuts his laptop and quickly takes Josh's place. The room is completely chaotic. I can't think. Everyone seems to be running around, but they're all going in super slow motion. Or maybe that's just how it looks to me.

"Blade! Grab him!"

Our heads all snap over to Erik when his voice thunders over the chaos. My eyes widen as I watch Blade drag Seth back into the room from where he was attempting to slide out the door with a huge smirk on his face.

What the hell? Seth? What's he doing?

Seth struggles against him, trying to shove him away, but Blade is a mammoth of a man. He's twice my size. Seth, who doesn't have a lot of muscle and might be five feet ten if he's lucky, has no chance. Especially when Ace and Josh get involved.

Erik strides to their side and grabs Seth by the throat, slamming him back against the wall. "Seriously, motherfucker? You think I didn't fucking have suspicions about you? And you come in here thinking you'll be able to pull the wool over all their eyes? What the fuck did you poison him with? Huh?"

"Poison?" I croak out and look at my unconscious boyfriend. I've surpassed terrified. I might throw up. Going to. I'm going to throw up.

"Lance! Get them to the bedroom!" Josh commands.

I jump but am spurred into action. I practically run. "Shouldn't someone call for help?" I ask. "I'll do it." I reach for my phone, trying to force myself to think clearly.

"Josh has it," Lance says. "Just trust him. Trust me. He's got it."

I nod as we lay Colton on the bed. "Fuck, he doesn't look good." I swallow hard. He's sweating. That has to be good, right? Dead people don't sweat. I mentally slap myself. He's not dead. He can't die. Not like this.

Not fucking like this.

"Go get a bowl with cold water and a cloth," Lance directs. I thank fuck my cousins followed us because I'm not moving.

Kody comes back a few moments later and hands Lance the cloth and bowl. "I got it as cold as I could, but I can get ice."

Lance shakes his head. "No. We're cooling him down. He's burning up. But we can't shock his system like that." He looks up at me.

76

"You need to help me get his clothes off. Pick someone you trust to see him naked because we're going to need help."

I just stare at him. I can't speak. I don't know if I'm breathing or breathing too much, but no words are coming out of my mouth. I trust all of my cousins. There's nothing in this world that I wouldn't trust them with, including my life and Colton's.

"Me," Brant says. He turns to Sterling. "Take the girls to the other bedroom. Kody, go with him to help keep them calm. He'll need the help. Where's Drake?"

"With Blade," Sterling says. "I don't think we'd pry him away even if this shit wasn't going to be his life."

I nod because I can't do anything else and meet Brant's eyes. I'm fucking grateful for him being able to take control and lead the team as well as I can, but I'm even more thankful that he can do the same thing off the field.

I can't breathe.

I can't even think.

Sterling and Kody usher Dylan and Rosie to the other room. Brant helps sit Colton up. I feel tears in my eyes as I wrestle with dead weight to get his clothes off of him while Lance jogs to Colton's private bathroom. I hear water running. It sets off my own waterfall of emotion. I never cry. I've broken bones and not cried.

But holy fuck do I do it now. I swipe at my eyes to get them to stop long enough for me to finish getting Colton's clothes off. His skin is pale. Clammy. He's cold to the touch, but he's sweating so badly that the clothes I just peeled off of him are soaked as badly as the sheets underneath him.

"Pull it together, Cap," Brant says. "He needs that tough as fuck quarterback strength right now. He'll be okay. I feel it."

I take a few deep breaths and help Brant get Colton up. I will the tears to stop as we fight to get him to the bathroom. Colton may be the most ripped man I've ever seen in my life, but all of that muscle on his two-hundred-twenty pound frame isn't easy to carry around. I thought I was strong, but I'm questioning my own strength, physical and otherwise, right now.

As soon as we get him into the bathroom, Lance takes over once more. "We're going to lift him into the tub. It'll help him cool down, but we need to make sure he doesn't go under. Best way to do that is someone behind him to hold him up, but we can't do that because we don't need anyone else's body heat affecting his. So, Xavier, You'll have to get behind him the best way you can."

I look at the tub. "It's against the wall. How?"

"On your knees at the side or sit on the edge. However you do it, it needs to be comfortable for you because you might be there for a while." Lance looks around. "Thermometer. Need to keep track of his temp."

"He's really organized. Probably the medicine cabinet," I say with a sniffle.

Lance nods before helping Brant and I lift Colton into the bath. When we have him settled, I make myself comfortable and hold him up. The water doesn't seem to be cold enough, but I trust Lance. I don't know what to do in this situation, so I allow him the lead.

I'm barely aware of Dylan and Rosie entering the room, Kody and Sterling right behind them, with arms full of linens. They head straight for the bed and start stripping it. The four of them work together to remake the bed. Dylan grabs new clothing for Colton while Rosie throws his old ones in a pile with his sheets. Kody picks everything up and moves out of the room while Sterling finishes with the bed. Almost as quickly as they came in, they're gone.

I drop my head to Colton's shoulder. "Come on, baby. You can't leave me like this. I just got you."

Lance pops the thermometer in Colton's mouth and looks up at Brant. "Go get the cloth and bowl. We need to use it on his neck and face."

Brant does as he's told, returning seconds later. Lance pulls the thermometer out of Colton's mouth when it beeps. With a nod, he turns on the cold water and pulls the plug. He lets the water cool more before replacing the plug and letting the level fill slightly. He shuts the cool water off as I look up at him.

"What now?" I ask over the ball forming in my throat.

"We wait," he says.

I nod and kiss Colton's cheek and the corner of his mouth. I hold him close while keeping his head above water. Brant continues using the cloth on his head and face. Lance keeps checking his temperature.

But Colton doesn't wake up.

☪ ☪ ☪

I keep using the cool cloth on Colton's face and checking the ice pack on the back of his neck. I'm being very careful not to get too close to him so my body heat doesn't make his go up, but it's not easy. I want to hold him close and heal him with all of the love I have for him. I know we technically just began our relationship, but in my eyes I've been falling in love with him for months. Last night was just us admitting what we've both already known, and taking the next step in the relationship we've already established.

I run my fingers through his hair. It's still damp from the sweat, but his fever did break a few hours ago. He still hasn't woken up, though. The doctor said the antidote he gave him to counteract the poison would take a while to really work.

Apparently, it was some kind of venom. Something that Colton couldn't taste or smell. It was colorless. I'm not sure of all of the details, but I really don't care about them. All I care about is how sick he is; if he'll make it through this. The doctor says he'll be fine, but I've refused to allow him to leave this penthouse. If something happens and Colton takes a turn, I want him here.

I look up at the quiet knock on the door. I asked everyone to leave us be when the doctor showed and was done with him. Brant was hesitant, but he listened. I just need to be alone with Colton. They all understood that, as I knew they would. Though, they've all checked in over the day.

"Yeah?" I croak out. I didn't realize how dry my throat was.

Drake pokes his head in with a glass of something cold that's filled with ice. "I brought you a Dew. Thought you could use it. Also, I wanted to let you know what we've found out about what happened."

I take the glass he hands me and take a long drink before handing it back to him. He puts it on the nightstand next to the bed as he sits down. "How is he?"

I look down at Colton. "He's getting his color back. The sweats have stopped. He's breathing just fine, but he's still out."

"He'll wake up, X. I don't know him well, but I know he's fucking stubborn as fuck. Just by what you've told us. He'll want to get his hands on the fucker who did this to him. Though, that's not happening." He chuckles a little darkly. "Blade and Ace took him to Viper's Ranch."

I chuckle, but there's no emotion behind it. The truth is, I really don't give a shit. "All I care about is Colton."

"Fuck, X." He reaches over and squeezes my shoulder. "I know."

I reach over and dip the cloth in the bowl of cold water I just refilled and ring it out. "It's been hours. Scares the fuck out of me. I just got him, Drake." I gently put the cloth on Colton's head.

"Fuck… That's… cold…," Colton murmurs.

I jerk back my arm. My heart leaps into my throat. "Colt?"

He doesn't open his eyes, but a smile slowly turns up one corner of his mouth. "Hey, baby."

"Christ, Colt. I thought I'd lost you."

"That's not happening." He shifts his arm slightly with a groan and wraps it around me. Drake runs out the door calling for the doctor. Colton pulls me into him, but I can feel how weak he is. "I'm still here."

"Barely," I whisper, cuddling into his chest.

The next few minutes are a flurry of motion. The doctor comes in and checks Colton out. Erik comes in to check on his friend. Josh and Lance come in just to make sure things are going smoothly. My cousins come in and make sure we're both doing okay. Erik and I help Colton sit up. The doctor allows him water through a straw. When everything settles, the only ones left in the room are me and Erik, per Colton's request.

I kiss his shoulder as I push his hair back. "I'm so happy you're okay."

"Just a little on the weak side." He turns and kisses the top of my head. I put an arm around his waist. I let myself relax a little and just feel him.

He soothingly runs his fingers through my hair. "What happened?" Colton asks. "Last thing I remember was standing up to go to bed with a massive fucking headache."

Erik nods slowly with a dark glare and chuckles a little. "Fucker came after you. Seth."

Colton raises an eyebrow. "Why?"

"Wasn't sure at first. I got suspicious, though, because he was always around your drinks. Coffee. Water. I didn't see him doing anything, but I did catch him shoving something in his pocket at one point. Didn't know what it was, but that's when I gave you a bottle of water instead of the glass he handed you. Your headache improved a bit. You'd gone to the bathroom a few times. It was like you were coming out of a fog."

He nods slowly and winces a little. "I remember feeling better with the bottled water, but I didn't put two and two together. I thought I just needed water and coffee wasn't agreeing with me or something."

"I kept an eye on you. Especially after I came back from the bathroom and you'd downed another glass of water. It was your second glass. I wanted to see what it did. You started to look more and more tired. I'd already decided to have the glass tested and talk to Seth about what I saw and his fucking attitude about you not drinking from the glasses. I was going to do it as soon as Josh was done talking, but things happened quickly. You were on your feet wanting to go to bed. Then, you passed out."

"All I remember is feeling like I needed to go to the bedroom."

"Well, I wasn't the only one who noticed. Xavier saw a few red flags, but didn't know what to make of them. He thought you were acting a little off. Not as alert. Even though you were tired. He knows you've gone without sleep and weren't affected like that. Josh said he'd started helping you with breakfast because you were stumbling. Blade pulled me aside and asked me if you were okay. You just didn't seem like you."

I shift a little and look at him. "Your skin is returning to a normal color. But if you think I'll stop fussing over you, you'd better think again."

Colton chuckles and pulls me closer until his lips are just brushing mine. "I wouldn't have it any other way. I'll never admit it to another soul, but I like you taking care of me." He smiles as he kisses me.

Erik chuckles. "You realize there's a witness. Right here." He waves his hand when Colton pulls away with a grin. I laugh. Erik smiles. "See?"

"Yeah, but you'll have my back. Keep my secrets," Colton says. "Always have."

"Always will." Erik pats Colton's leg lightly.

As he continues filling Colton in on everything that went on out there, I can't help but tune it all out. I settle against Colton's chest and close my eyes. His heartbeat, strong and true, along with his hand running up and down my arm calm me more.

It's crazy and far scarier than I'm willing to admit, but I almost lost him today. It's a thought that's run through my mind so many times and chills me to my core. I'd almost completely forgotten about everything else going on, including my father and how he's in the hands of Viper's Venom.

If I'm being honest with myself, I have no doubts that this is just the beginning. I'm sure all what happened today was just a blip on the highlight reel.

Questions still need to be answered.

People need to be dealt with.

The city is about to go through an intense shake-up.

I just hope to fuck that we all come out on the other side unscathed.

Epilogue

☪ Colton ☪

(Three Weeks Later)

I lean against the bleachers at the high school behind where the players sit with a huge smile plastered to my face. Xavier led his team to the playoffs. Despite all the shit we've gone through over the past couple of months, and me recovering from being poisoned, Xavier has shined both on and off the field. He's taken care of me, his cousins, and this team. I can see why he's the number one ranked high school quarterback in the state right now. He's broken records, so the talk of him being the best of all time holds a lot of merit. I couldn't be more fucking proud.

I clap and whistle when Xavier throws an ace of a pass that gets the team a first down. Not so sure they need it. It's just coming up on halftime. The Bullhorns are up by twenty-one points. The other team has yet to score. It's a complete slaughter.

I can't believe how much has happened in just three weeks. The Viper's Venom got a lot of information from Xavier's dad about the gambling ring. Turns out, Seth was the head of it. He didn't like that I'd gotten so close to it. He thought if he took me out, that would be the end of it.

But he fucked up.

Twice.

Firstly, he didn't put enough poison in my water. His intention wasn't to make me sick. It was to kill me, but he didn't use the poison correctly. He also didn't count on Erik noticing what was going on and giving me bottles instead of the glasses that he kept putting out for me.

And secondly, he didn't count on me calling in the mafia or a biker's crew to help me out. Even when they showed up, he underestimated them on all levels. He'd heard of the Lucinio Mafia, but he never believed just how powerful they are. And he had no idea how closely they work with Viper's Venom or the police when we ask them.

Too bad for him, really. But it doesn't really matter now. He's been taken care of. Cops don't do well in prison. He's still awaiting trial, but I heard he may have had the shit beat out of him, and that the guards stood by and watched it all go down. I don't feel an ounce of sympathy. Not after all the shit he's done. Right up to murder in his sick and twisted snake bite games. Viper's could have finished him off, but we all agreed he'd have a lot more fun with their allies, guards and cons alike, in prison.

We also found out the reason that Xavier was pushed so hard into going to A&M is because his dad made an agreement with Seth and his partners, who Josh and his crew have all so nicely hunted down for me. The deal involved getting all of his debt wiped clean so long as his son played nice and did what he was told.

Xavier was supposed to become the starting quarterback. His dad would tell him to either win or lose the game. In return, Xavier wouldn't have to worry about school in the slightest. His grades and everything would be bought and paid for. Essentially, my theory wasn't that far off. He thought he could make his son do whatever he wanted. I suppose he didn't think Xavier would stand up for himself. What started out simply as a father who wanted his son to follow in his footsteps turned into something far more sinister.

While Seth ended up in prison and his partners won't be heard from again, Xavier's father has to live with the fact that he fucked up so badly that he lost it all. He was fired from the department, along with several other dirty cops, because he was involved in a lot of the gambling.

He'll probably spend some time in prison himself because of just how much he let happen, like the murder of innocent men, without saying anything to anyone. Charges of conspiracy and accessory to murder have been filed against him. He's out on bail. He's not only lost his job, but also his entire family, though. Xavier's mother left him. Can't blame her.

I'm a little bit surprised to see her here with Brant's father and step-mother. She's starting life on her own, but she's recovering from a lot of shit from what I understand. Mental abuse, emotional trauma, and a drug and drinking problem. Xavier left just in the nick of time, in my opinion. He avoided the entire implosion. At least most of it.

Josh Lucinio has done a damn good job of cleaning up this city. True to his word, I've gotten all of the credit and will continue to. Command staff in my own department have gone down. City officials, including the Mayor, have been caught up in the chaos. It's only the beginning. He'll be leaving behind two of his best guys, Lance and Damon, to help with the fallout. Tomorrow night, another key and very high up player in all of this shit will be taken out.

And that's not the only thing that we're caught up in. The teacher who assaulted Rosie may have been caught, but her mother has gone missing over the last three weeks. So have a couple of men from Viper's Venom. It looks like suspicions of them trying to overthrow Blade are correct. What they didn't count on, though, is Blade's close ties to other Chapters of Viper's Venom, including the fucking President of the entire crew himself. Alec, in order to help, has not only left Ink here, but he's also personally flying back and forth from Chicago when he's needed.

With all of the assistance we're getting here, I'm sure it won't be long before the mystery surrounding Rosie's family is solved. Dylan's mom got pretty sick of having Rosie around and complained just enough to make Rosie feel like a burden. Xavier told her she could stay with us, but Damon and Lance offered to keep her with them instead. Rosie agreed because it's more protection for her, even though she's pretty convinced she doesn't need it.

I know she has gotten close to them both. They took the time to make sure she was comfortable and understood everything that has been going on. She didn't say it, but I could see in her body language that she was happy to be living with them. I can't say I'm not relieved about it. With rogue Viper's Venom members involved, she'll need all the protection she can get. She wants to go back to Huckleberry Grove. She misses it.

"Yeah! Go, Xavier!" I yell as he starts running for the end zone instead of passing. I don't see anyone open. The decision to run was a good one.

The crowd erupts in thunderous cheers when he scores the touchdown for his team and brings us into halftime. His teammates hug him as everyone starts jogging off the field. Xavier makes his way straight to me.

"Hey, Detective Fuckable. Did you see that play?"

"Hell yeah, I did." I wrap him in my arms when he reaches me and kiss him long and deeply. One thing I've come to love about him is that he isn't afraid to show us off. He doesn't give a fuck who sees us together. He's just as proud of our relationship as I am.

"Damn, you taste good," he says to me when I pull away.

I grin. "So do you." I tap his ass. "Get your ass in the locker room. Your team needs you to rally them to victory."

He laughs. "You seen the scoreboard?" He gives me a quick peck to the lips as he turns and jogs away. "Love you!"

"Love you, too!" I call after him as my heart swells. I really do fucking love him.

I watch him disappear as he makes his way into the school and catch sight of Dylan. I raise an eyebrow. She slowly makes her way behind her squad to their locker room. She looks a little like she wants to cry.

"You okay, sweetie?" I ask her when she walks by me.

She jumps a little as she looks at me and shakes her head. "I heard a weird phone call earlier." She looks down. "I've been obsessing over it."

"What phone call? Who was involved?"

She shrugs. "It was just my dad. He said something like she'll never know. I got the feeling he was talking about me. He just seems so secretive lately." She shakes her head like she's trying to shrug it off. "I'm sure it's nothing."

I hold out my arms and fold her in a hug when she steps into them. "I know you're dad loves the fuck out of you. Maybe whatever it is has nothing to do with you, but I also know you need to follow your instincts, sweetheart." I kiss the top of her head as I release her. "It might be nothing, but it might not be. Just keep your eyes open. Hell, maybe he's planning a surprise party for you."

She giggles and smiles. "Maybe you're right. My birthday is coming up soon."

I smile. "See? You never know."

"Thanks, Colton."

"Anytime, honey."

I smile as she jogs after her squad. I move off to the side more as people start passing me to head for the concession stand. I decide to follow because a Coke and nachos doesn't sound bad at all. Even if the line is long.

"Sloane, wait!"

I turn and see Brant grabbing the arm of a girl who might be half his size. I recognize her as his stepmom. I've only seen her a couple of times. Once was at her wedding. Brant's dad invited the entire department. I hadn't intended to go, but I ended up doing it because a friend needed a date. She didn't want to go alone and get hit on.

Sloane's very petite. She's not all that tall. Her hair is dark. She looks like she's been crying. I know whatever's going on is probably private, but I can't look away. Brant pulls her back from the line a little bit, but they're still close enough to me that I can hear them. Even though they're not talking all that loudly.

"I don't belong here, Brant," she says quietly. She looks past him and shakes her head. "I shouldn't have come."

"Sloane, come on. Don't let him fuck with you like this. This is a huge game for us. I don't get to play running back much because I'm backup for X. To get to play in a game like this is huge. I asked you to come because I want you here. He doesn't matter."

"But he does, Brant. Don't you see? He'll just make things difficult for me if I disobey him and stay. I'm not part of this world." She sniffles. "I never will be." She pulls away from him and runs towards the parking lot.

Brant looks after her sadly but doesn't run after her. I'm just about to ask him what that was all about, but I don't get the opportunity because he turns around with his head down and walks towards the school to join his team. I thought he didn't get along well with his stepmother, but the look he just gave her tells a far different story.

After I finally get my snacks, I make my way back to the field and find a seat this time. Not that I mind standing. It gives me a good view of Xavier. Nothing to be upset about there. But I find a seat next to Blade just as the team starts coming back to the field. I stay standing long enough for Xavier to see where I am.

"Didn't think you were going to get here," Blade says when I sit next to him.

I smile. "I've been here. I was a little late, but I saw the touchdown pass just before Xavier ran for their last touchdown. Fourteen points in like two minutes. Not bad."

Blade laughs. "Drake's catch was something to be proud of. Jerry Rice or Chris Carter shit right there."

I grin. "That catch was fucking phenomenal. One-handed. Just plucked out of the fucking air like it was nothing."

"He's a damn good player."

"Probably why all the colleges want him."

He smiles proudly. "Too bad he's already committed to BSU."

"So, it'll be Drake as receiver, Brant as running back and then Sterling and Kody? Fuck. They'll be unstoppable."

"I see a contender for the top spot." Blade steals one of my loaded nachos. "Championships for sure."

I smile widely because I know he's right. These guys are called the Dream Team. Brystone Springs hasn't had a championship team like this ever. They've won championships, but never with a team this good.

They're special.

☪ ☪ ☪

"I think we'll have to turn the guest bedroom into a trophy room," I say with a proud grin as we walk past the room hand in hand.

Xavier laughs. "With the amount of trophies I plan on winning in my life? It won't be big enough. We'll have to move."

"I'd move anywhere you asked me to if it meant you following your dreams and being happy, baby. Except overseas. I'd prefer to keep my feet on United States soil."

He tugs my hand and pushes me against the wall near our bedroom. "My plans don't include overseas football. Do they even call it that?" He presses his body against mine with a wicked grin and glint in his eye.

I groan and wrap my arms around his waist. "Rugby."

He shakes his head. "Ain't the same. Weird uniforms. Not as popular as soccer."

"Football," I say teasingly, pulling him closer.

He makes a face. "It's soccer. Europeans don't know what football is."

I laugh because I know he's kidding. He'll watch a Chelsea FC game with me all day and love every second. He gets just as into it. He throws popcorn, chips, or even candy at the screen when there's a foul or a shit call. Penalty shootouts typically have us both clutching our chests and panicking as we wait. Penalties in a normal or championship game are stressful enough. But penalty shootouts at a World Cup game after extra time? Fuck me. Call me a doctor.

We may need to find a way to protect the TV when we watch next year's World Cup. Xavier and I invited everyone to our penthouse to watch it with us. Somehow, the TV ended up with a smashed screen after Blade threw his glass at it in outrage when the referee made a bad call. Something about how the player had made a dirty tackle. But we all agreed we didn't see any issue with the foul. It looked clean to us.

I let my hands wander under his t-shirt and up his back. "You played a really good game. Kicked ass. I don't think I've ever seen a team obliterate another team in a game like that."

If I didn't know Xavier, I'd say he's preening under the praise and blushing. But I don't have much time to really play around with that idea because his lips are crashing into mine in a hungry kiss that leaves me breathless and hard as a steel in seconds.

When his fingertips find the waistband of my jeans, it's all over. I deepen the kiss and grip his ass. I push off the wall and back him into our bedroom without breaking it. At least not until the backs of his knees hit the bed.

I nip his lip as I pull away and push him backwards onto the bed. He looks up at me, a little wide-eyed at the aggression and growl I let out, with a sexy smirk that makes me want to tear his clothes off.

So, I do.

I peel off his shirt, then pants, then boxer briefs until he's bare-ass naked in front of me. I quickly remove mine and crawl into the bed, shifting us so we're both more comfortable. Xavier pushes me on my back with heated lust in his eyes and leans down. He kisses me long and hard, tangling his tongue with mine, as he straddles me.

Xavier has always been a top. He's never taken dick. Always been the one to give it. So, when he allowed me to claim his ass, our relationship catapulted from the just exploring each other stage to the we're going to get married because we don't want anyone else.

Xavier is all mine. Just like I'm his.

I let my head fall back with a moan and gasp when he lowers himself over my dick. "Fuck… Xavier."

His ass pulses around my cock. He doesn't even give himself time to adjust to my size before he's moving back and forth on me. I grip his hips as he sits up and rests his hands on my stomach. I'm sure most would have their eyes glued to his dick. Xavier's big. Maybe not my size, but he's big.

His dick, though, isn't what has my attention. It's the fact that his ass is taking all of me. I'm buried balls deep. It's astonishing how well someone who has always done the fucking, never been fucked, can take a guy like me as well as he does.

I start thrusting, but it's not long before Xavier is riding me like a fucking rodeo bull. I always like to be the one in control. It's just not like that with him, though. Neither of us are in control. We just feel and do what's right for us.

Xavier starts clenching around me as he moves back and forth over me while he bounces. He closes his eyes. "Oh fuck. Colt! Don't stop. Don't stop!"

He leans back and grips my thighs. It's my cue that he's done with the ride. So, I give him what he wants. I brace my feet on the bed and grip his hips as I give him the fast, hard, and deep thrusts that he's come to love. I slap his ass with both hands, then grip his hips again, slamming him down so he's meeting my thrusts.

He reaches around to his dick as it slaps up and down. He grips it as I thrust and starts jerking it in time to my punishing pace. I'd stop him and stroke him myself. I love doing that. But one of my favorite things to do is watch him do it while I'm chasing both of our releases. The look of pleasure he gets on his face as I'm thrusting and he's stroking is something I'll never tire of. It makes me harder for him. Thicker.

I thrust faster with a grunt. "Christ, baby. You look so damn good jerking that cock of yours."

He smiles, but doesn't look down at me. "I know you like watching." He clenches around my dick and jerks his hips when I push my cock as deep inside him as I can. "Fuck!"

A shiver goes down my spine. My cock feels like it might break off if I don't come. My stomach clenches in anticipation. My spine tightens. His thighs tremble. My fingers grip his flesh tighter. I want so badly to let go, but I'll never do that if he's not there first.

"Come, Xavier," I moan as I give into my temptation. I reach for his balls and roll them in my palm. "Now." I tug on them.

"Oh fuck!" As soon as his release hits my stomach, I thrust hard into him a couple of more times.

"Holy shit… Yes!" The tightness in my spine erupts into a jolt of electricity that shoots straight to my cock. I come deep inside him, keeping his ass flush against my hips as I arch.

"Colton!" He spasms hard around me as my dick jerks inside him. He releases more onto my stomach, nearly collapsing.

"Xavier!" His balls, hard just moments ago, become putty in my hand as he gives me everything he has. I keep gently massaging them.

Several minutes later, after we've both come down and cleaned up, I pull Xavier into my side. As I think of how far we've come in such a short amount of time, I run my fingers through his hair. I never really thought I'd be here. I'm not the kind of man who expected to ever have a happily ever after. Especially with a guy who's twenty years younger than me. He's so far out of my league, it's laughable.

But here I am.

"I love you, Colton," Xavier murmurs as his breathing evens.

"I love you, too, baby," I whisper as I kiss his forehead.

And I do. With all my heart and soul, I love Xavier Remington. Forbidden to me on so many levels. Age. The fact that he's still a high school student. Most of all, because he still has his entire life in front of him. I'm happy to be a part of watching him take the world on.

But it's the fact that he loves me back that's the greatest gift of all.

The End

Bonus Chapter!

☾ Xavier ☾

(One Month Later)

"Hustle out there!" I shout enthusiastically to my team in our huddle. "We're in the championship game! We're not going to lose! We haven't lost a damn game yet. We're not starting now!" I look up at the scoreboard as my team shouts a chorus of agreement. "We have less than ten seconds to get out there and show everyone why we're here! Why we're the team to beat!"

"Fourth quarter," one of my younger guys says nervously. "You sure going for the fourth down is wise? We could just kick the field goal and win."

He's right. We're only down by one point. But that isn't the way I work. I shake my head. "We could. Or we could show everyone out there that we have the fucking guts to take this game all the way. And that's what we're going to do!" A whistle blows, signaling the end of the timeout I called. I look at the coach. "We're going for it. I'm handing the ball to Brant. Keep special teams off the field."

"Your game. Your team," Coach tells me. "Get out there!"

"Break!" I call as I clap my hands. The team runs out to the field and gets in position.

The crowd that's gathered for this game is loud. We're playing in the AT&T Stadium in Arlington, Texas. The very same one that my favorite NFL football team plays. Dallas Cowboys. It's my dream to play for them someday.

I'm on the right track. I don't have a doubt in my mind that I can make that dream a reality.

Especially with the level of support I have. My cousins and Colton are always in my corner, but I think the entire town came out to support us. Hell, maybe the State. The stadium is damn near filled. The cheering is deafening.

It's perfect.

I keep my eye on the play clock. "Green eighteen!" I yell to my team. I only yell it when I'm about to run a running play. I watch with a smirk as the defensive line adjusts. They think I'm about to throw a deep pass. It's exactly what I want them to think. "Green eighteen!" I yell again. I watch the clock countdown to two. "Hit!"

The ball snaps to me. I take two steps back as I turn. I hand the ball to Brant just as he runs behind me while my line blocks for me. I quickly turn like I still have the ball in my hand. Once I get to my pocket, I look around the field like I'm looking for a receiver.

Brant breaks through the line and takes off running down the field. I watch with a stupid grin as the crowd erupts in thunderous cheers. Brant is fucking fast. If he gets loose, no one is catching him. This time is no exception.

I grin and jog down the field after the rest of the team. "Go, Brant! Go! Run!" I yell from down the field.

Brant jumps so gracefully over someone trying to tackle him that I question if he might be a fucking deer. Or maybe a ballerina.

Five yards.

Four.

Three.

A defender barrels at him, but one of our players blocks him.

Two yards.

Someone breaks free of one of our blockers and sprints after Brant.

One yard.

The defender gets a hand on Brant's back. Brant keeps pushing and crosses into the endzone.

"Touchdown!" I scream as I break into a run. I glance up at the clock and see there are still two seconds left, but I don't care. No way our defensive line is letting these assholes score a touchdown or get anywhere near an area they can score.

I wrap my arms around Brant and a few other guys already hugging him when I reach them. We're all cheering but can't hear ourselves over the thunderous applause.

"Holy shit! We did it!" one of our rookies screams.

"Not yet, we didn't," Brant says as we all jog off the field.

A few moments later, our special teams is running onto the field to kick our extra point. I grab my water bottle from the hand of one of the Freshman who helps the team with towels and shit as I take off my helmet. My eyes don't leave the field.

Our kicker lines up his shot. The play clock ticks down the seconds. I can hear my heartbeat in my ears. I know we're ahead, but I always get complete tunnel vision when my guys are out there. I watch each move every single one of them make. If a play goes wrong or goes off without a hitch, I'm able to give feedback about what went wrong or right.

I bend and put my hands on my knees. The guys behind me are already cheering and celebrating the win, but two seconds is a lot of time to make something happen. I ignore the few pats on the back I get and stay focused.

The snap.

The position of the ball before the kick.

The kick.

Beaut-

"No!" I yell at the same time as Coach.

"No! Fuck!" Brant yells next to me.

I stand to my full height with my hands gripping my hair. I watch in horror as someone jumps up and blocks the otherwise perfect kick. He somehow hangs onto the ball and starts running for their endzone.

"Go! Fucking run!" I scream at the team. It's like they're all standing in shock and forgot to do anything. "Go! Get the fucking ball!"

"Move it! Catch him!" Coach yells. "Go! Go!"

As if our voices snap them out of their daydream, the line begins to move. One of our guys jump over a few people who have blocked a couple of other players. My heart jumps into my throat as I take off down the sidelines behind Coach.

"Who is that?" I yell. I can't see his number.

"Kody!" Brant yells from behind me.

"Go! Kody, run!" I scream as we make our way down the sideline. I completely forgot that Kody was filling in for one of our guys who was injured. He doesn't usually play on our special teams.

The guy is wide open. No one is in front of him. But there's a reason Kody is an All-Star. It's because he's good and just as fast as Brant. There may be no one in front of the asshole from the other team, but there's also no one behind him to block him from Kody.

Kody pumps his legs even faster until he's in striking distance. The guy looks over his shoulder just as he reaches the ten yard line. I can see him start to run faster, but there's no use. Kody tackles him to the ground. The ball comes loose.

My eyes widen. "Ball! Ball!" I yell, jumping up and down like a maniac. "Ball! Kody, ball!"

The other guys are gaining fast. Kody, reacting quickly, pushes himself up enough to leap onto the ball just as several defenders reach him. He tucks the ball quickly under him as two guys pounce.

"Yeah!" I jump up and down. The time on the scoreboard is at zero. I run with the rest of our team onto the field as the whistle blows to signal the end of the game. I reach Kody just as he's being pulled to his feet by one of our guys. "Yeah!" I wrap him in a bear hug, lifting him clean off his feet.

"Christ, X." Kody laughs as I hug him.

The other guys gather around us and lift Kody on their shoulders. It looks like confetti is raining down around us. Must have confetti guns somewhere. We carry Kody around the field as the crowd completely loses their collective minds. Some of them are even running to the field.

But my eyes are on one man.

Colton.

We all put Kody down just as Colton reaches us. He wraps his arms around me. Others embrace the other players. There's a lot of patting me on the back, congratulations, screaming, and yelling, but the only thing I hear is Colton's voice.

"Holy fuck, I'm so proud of you, baby. That was a hell of a game.

I thought you were done at halftime when you hurt your ankle. You okay?" He hugs me even tighter.

I smile into his neck. "It's wrapped up pretty good. I wasn't going to miss the game."

He chuckles with a low rumble. "I'll take care of it and you later."

"I look forward to it, Detective Insatiable." I grin against his neck as he lets me go.

He nods to where the team is gathering for the presentation of the trophy. It's too bad the school gets to keep it, but I'm getting a replica made for me and the entire team. Smaller and cheaper versions, but trophies nonetheless.

I plan to remember and memorialize this game for all of us forever. It was hard fought, and we put all of our hearts and souls into it.

I jog towards the center of the field with a huge grin on my face and a lot of pride for my team in my heart.

☪ ☪ ☪

(Five Days Later)

"The biggest problem is that I don't fucking get this," Colton says. He leans back against the couch he's sitting in and locks his hands behind his head. He looks at Lance, one of the guys left behind last month by Josh Lucinio, leader of the Lucinio Mafia, and gestures to the map he spread out on the coffee table. "I was hoping you would."

Lance leans forward and studies the map. It's of the entire State of Texas. I haven't looked too much at it. All I know is it has a lot of marks and has something to do with Blade and his crew. The dude who disappeared. Twitch or some shit. I guess the name comes from when he was a prospect. He was jittery and twitchy. Always watching everyone else. Quiet. Didn't talk a lot.

I walk from the kitchen to the living room with drinks for Damon, Lance, me, and Colton. They all take them gratefully as I sit. Colton has been pouring over this map for hours, but I know he had it at the department. He took it home because he decided he needed help. He's been so lost in it, he's barely explained to me or them what the hell it is.

I sit down next to him. Time to help him out. Organize his wayward thoughts. "So, other than dealing with this Twitch dude, what is all this about?" I ask, leaning into Colton.

He gives me a grateful smile as he takes a long drink of his Coke. He sets the glass down as he leans forward. "This is a map of all the places Twitch has been spotted around Texas. The dates of each sighting are written on the map next to the red mark that indicates where he was seen. He zigzags back and forth. It doesn't make fucking sense. What the hell is he doing?"

Lance tilts his head and takes out his laptop. "Let me just input this."

Damon takes out his phone. "Just gonna take some pics."

I lean forward and look at the dates. I follow them with my eyes. I furrow my brows and huff out a breath as I tilt my head. "I don't know if I'm imagining this, but..." I trail off and start tracing the pattern I see, starting from the first date.

Colton looks at me with a raised eyebrow before turning back to my finger and watching me. "What are you seeing?"

"Well, it looks like... almost... a name or something." I keep tracing. "See? This would be an E. Here's a T. It's connected, but here's a H. Then an A. And this last one would be..."

"A N. It's a N," Damon says. "Holy shit." He looks up at Lance as he sits back in his chair. "That can't be fucking possible. Can it?"

"What?" Colton asks. "Who's Ethan? What am I missing here?"

Lance let's a breath and pinches the bridge of his nose. "Ethan. Ethan Crane is Josh's uncle. Josh's father, Matthew Lucinio, had a huge rivalry with Ethan Crane for years. They had a long and complicated history that would take hours to unravel. We killed him. He's dead. And we made fucking sure of it. This doesn't make sense."

"Well, many people in the world are named Ethan, right?" Colton asks. "It doesn't necessarily mean Ethan Crane."

"We've learned not to believe in coincidence," Damon says. "And I know you don't believe in coincidence either. Whatever this is, there's a reason for it. We need to figure this out and fast."

Colton puts a hand on my leg and smiles. "How did you see that so quickly? I've been staring at this map for days."

"I'm a quarterback. Seeing patterns is kind of in my job

description." I give him a smile, but I can't say I'm not a bit nervous at this news.

Colton rubs his hand up and down my back. I know he's trying to soothe me, but I can't help wondering what's to come. Even though my future with Colton is as sure as the sun will rise in the morning, everything seems uncertain.

No matter what happens in the coming days, weeks, months, and years, though, I know the bond I have with Colton and my cousins will remain. Whatever happens will happen.

And we'll get through it together.

Next In The Forbidden Temptation Series

The Forbidden Temptation Series continues with *The Running Back's Forbidden Temptation*.

When my father married Sloane, I vowed to hate her. I have a mother. Well…, had. I had a mother. A very good one who I'll always carry with me in my heart.

But that was three years ago. I was fifteen.

Since then, Sloane and I have come to realize two things. The first is that my father isn't the suave man we thought he was. The second is that I'm not the jerk that I tried to make her think I am.

Ever since I opened my eyes to the truth in front of me, I've been the one to build her up when my father tears her down. I've been the one to comfort her when he causes her emotional breakdowns.

I'd give her the entire world if she'd let me.

When I return for a visit just after leaving for college because I miss her, I discover that my father has done something unforgivable. Every protective fiber of my being is front and center. I make a decision that will change our lives.

Now, I just need to make Sloane see that her forever is with me.

Order *The Running Back's Forbidden Temptation* Today!

The Forbidden Temptation Series

Available Now

The Detective's Forbidden Temptation

Other Books By Melony Ann
The Beautiful Dream Series

Available Now

Loving You
My Love, My Heart
Softening Lyric
Undercover Temptations
Captain Charming
Breaking Boundaries
Crashing Into You
Tactical Inferno
Ravishing Our Queen
Cherished By The Texan
Unveiling Our Passions

Box Sets Available

The Beautiful Dream Series: Box Set: Part 1
The Beautiful Dream Series: Box Set: Part 2

The Crane Family Series

Available Now

The Reluctant Mafia King
Sweet Lies
Billion Dollar Love Story
Be Mine
Protecting Her
Dangerously Forbidden Love
His Heart
Love In The Dark

Box Sets Available

The Crane Family Series

The Deimos Trilogy

Available Now

Connor's Legacy
Aryan's Alpha
Kade's Redemption

Box Sets Available

The Deimos Trilogy

The Lucinio Family Series

Available Now

Rising From The Ashes
The Player's Rebel
Encrypting My Heart

Multi Author Series
Piper Falls: Firehouse 49

Available Now

Ignite My Fire by Melony Ann
Regain My Fire by Kindra White
Playing With My Fire by D.L. Howe
Fight My Fire by Darley Collins
Against My Fire by Anneke Boshoff
Relight My Fire by Louise Murchie
Harness My Fire by Ayana Lisbet
Quench My Fire by Havana Wilder

Let's Be Friends

Follow me on

Bookbub

Facebook

Goodreads

Instagram

Tik Tok

Visit my website
www.melonyannauthor.com

Subscribe to my newsletter and get a FREE never-seen-before NOVELLA
just for subscribers!
https://www.melonyannauthor.com/exclusive-content

Join my Facebook Reader Group!
Jason's and Melony's Sizzling Book Nook

The official Forbidden Temptation Series Playlist on YouTube
https://youtube.com/playlist?list=PLGEiD5wbQmDfSjcIbdaBUl79mqR6t
URPP

Dedication

When our wings are broken, you help us fly.
When we drift too close to the sun, you shield us.
When we flounder, you keep us afloat.

Acknowledgements

Brad - You're the guy I thought I could never have. The one way above my league. Imagine my surprise when you said you love me, too.

Laura - My pretty little temptation. My love. My world.

Jay - My heart; my soul belonged to you when your pretty jade eyes met mine. You still own all of me.

Kelly - I love that you're part of the family I got to choose.

Ayana - You're like a rare flower beautifully blooming in a sea of the mundane. I don't know what I'd do without you.

Anneke - I wish you were here. But you will be soon, and I can't wait!

Jason - When I doubt everything, you're the one guiding me out of my darkness.

To the Bookstagram Community.

To my family.

To all of those who believe in me and support me.

To all of those who don't.

Cover by: Carter Cover Designs

Edited by: Alyssa Skaggs

About Melony Ann

Melony Ann began writing short stories and poetry as a child. She continued honing her craft over the years until she took the plunge and began publishing her work, despite having severe anxiety.

Melony writes contemporary romance stories that are full of suspense and a lot of steam.

When she isn't writing, she is loving her family and working to make her life something she deserves.

Melony believes that if her writing can inspire just one person, then all of her hard work is worth it.

Her hope is that her writing allows each and every one of her readers to escape for a little while. To dive into a different world one book at a time.

www.ingramcontent.com/pod-product-compliance
Lightning Source LLC
Chambersburg PA
CBHW051307170626
46809CB00004B/1788